The Home School Detectives

THE MYSTERY OF THE
HOMELESS TREASURE

John Bibee

INTERVARSITY PRESS
DOWNERS GROVE, ILLINOIS 60515

© 1994 by John Bibee

All rights reserved. No part of this book may be reproduced in any form without written permission from InterVarsity Press, P.O. Box 1400, Downers Grove, IL 60515.

InterVarsity Press® is the book-publishing division of InterVarsity Christian Fellowship®, a student movement active on campus at hundreds of universities, colleges and schools of nursing in the United States of America, and a member movement of the International Fellowship of Evangelical Students. For information about local and regional activities, write Public Relations Dept., InterVarsity Christian Fellowship, 6400 Schroeder Rd., P.O. Box 7895, Madison, WI 53707-7895.

Cover illustration: David Darrow

ISBN 0-8308-1911-8

Printed in the United States of America

Library of Congress Cataloging-in-Publication has been requested.

15	14	13	12	11	10	9	8	7	6	5	4	3
05	04	03	02	01	00	99	98	97				

1. Lost _____ 5

2. The Golden Cup _____ 15

3. Mr. Finley's Antiques _____ 23

4. The Blue Van _____ 33

5. Robbed! _____ 43

6. Detectives in the Making_____ 52

7. Buried Treasure? _____ 61

8. A Fake Beard _____ 70

9. Break-In_____ 80

10. What Molly Found _____ 89

11. In the Cave_____ 99

12. Digging a Grave_____ 106

13. The Party Begins _____ 110

Chapter One

Lost

"What do you mean, 'Billy's missing'?" Josh Morgan asked.

"He's gone," Becky Renner said. She was Billy's twin sister. "I don't see his bike or anything."

"But I thought he was going to stick with you all."

"That was the plan." Julie Brown ran her hand through her long, dark hair to loosen a twig that had gotten caught in it.

"Then how could Billy be lost?" Josh frowned and kicked the dirt. He looked at the other kids. He was in charge since he was the oldest. The five kids sat on their bikes at the top of Lookout Bluff just beyond Springdale Cemetery. In the distance below, beyond Springdale Park, they could see the lake. Each of them was holding a paper sack. Inside the sacks were plastic bags with samples of leaves. Julie also carried her sketchbook in her backpack.

The six children had begun their leaf-collecting trip as part of a science project in their home school studies. Josh, age twelve, and Emily Morgan, age ten, were brother and sister. Both were blond, tall, athletic and good all-around students. Becky and Billy Renner were African-Americans, and ten-year-old twins. Billy was talkative and impulsive, while Becky was much more quiet and cautious. Julie and Carlos were brother and sister by adoption. Carlos, age ten, was born in Mexico, but his parents had died in a plane crash when he was two. Pastor Brown had been good friends with Carlos's parents and had adopted Carlos. Carlos had thick, straight black hair and a cheerful smile. Julie, age eleven, had long, dark hair like her mother and wore glasses like her father.

All three families home schooled, and they all were using the same science books. Since they were also part of a home school co-op in their church, they often took field trips together, or worked together on projects, like the leaf-collecting safari that afternoon. But more than that, they were neighbors and friends and shared a growing faith in God.

Josh had been planning to collect leaf samples along the edge of the lake after they had exhausted the different varieties in the cemetery and park. He was about to call the others all together when they realized Billy was gone.

"I don't see how he could just disappear," Josh said.

"We don't keep him on a leash, you know," Emily

protested. "Besides, you know how Billy is. He was running here and running there, stuffing leaves as fast as he could into his sack. I don't think he was even using his plastic sample bags."

"Of course, he wasn't," Carlos said. "Billy is always in a hurry."

"And he disappeared faster than a rabbit," Emily continued. "Julie and Becky and I stopped to read the old graves over in the corner of the cemetery. Did you know they have some graves marked simply as 'Unknown Man'? Can you imagine dying and no one even knowing your name?"

"They must have been strangers in town," Julie said softly. "That's sad. I made a sketch of the graves and the tree. I might come back and do a watercolor later."

Julie was always bringing home wounded or lost animals. The Brown family had three dogs, four cats, a turtle and a duck named Waggert. Julie had found the duck by the side of the road. Its leg had been broken and she had nursed it back to health. She wanted to be a veterinarian or an artist when she got older.

"But what about Billy?" Josh felt the need to get everyone back on track. Sometimes he liked being the unofficial leader of the group. But other times he felt like he was nothing more than a big baby sitter and he resented it, especially when things went wrong, like Billy disappearing. Josh began to feel a knot of fear mixed with anger growing inside.

"He's probably not lost," Carlos observed coolly. He wanted to be a scientist when he was older. "He knows this area extremely well. Still, it is possible that he could have hurt himself."

"Why me?" Josh muttered, trying to remain calm. He hated that feeling of not being sure what to do. He took a deep breath. "Let's think back over this. You guys stopped to read the gravestones. And Julie was drawing in her sketchpad."

"Right," Emily replied. "And before we knew it, he was gone. And so was Molly." Molly was the Renners' golden retriever. She always tagged along on all the outdoor field trips.

"Wait a minute." Josh turned in a circle. Then he put his hands up to his mouth and yelled, "Moooollyyyy! Moooollyyyy!"

"You could yell for Billy all day and he wouldn't come." Becky smiled. "But Molly knows her name."

"This could be serious, you guys." Josh turned around and yelled again. This time they all heard a dog bark. The sound came from down below the bluff.

They dropped their bikes and ran over near the edge of the bluff. The barking was louder.

"I can hear her but can't see her," Becky said. "Moll-lyy! Here girl!"

"Billy!" Josh called. Then his eyes stopped. On the ground near Carlos's feet he saw bicycle tracks running through the grass and weeds. The tracks disappeared over the edge of the bluff. "Bike tracks!"

The children ran to the edge of the bluff and stopped. The tracks continued down the extremely steep slope of the bluff through weeds and tall grass.

They stared at the tracks in silence at first.

"You don't think he tried riding down that slope on purpose do you?" Carlos asked.

"That is exactly the kind of thing Billy would do," Josh said. In an instant they were all running for the zigzag trail of stone steps that led down the side of the bluff into Springdale Park.

Josh was the first one down to the flat land below, followed by the others. They were all breathing hard.

"I see his bike!" Josh pointed. "Down by that big oak tree." They all ran for the bike. Just as they reached it, Josh shouted out. "Stop!" He held up his arms holding the others back. The bicycle was at the base of the oak tree, half covered by a large green patch of weeds.

"Is he hurt?" Becky thought Josh saw Billy lying on the ground. Josh shook his head and held up his arms. He pointed to the ground.

"What is it?" Becky pushed up beside him.

"Poison ivy," Josh said simply. A sea of poison ivy surrounded the base of the big oak tree. The other children stepped back. No one wanted to be itching for the next week. But there was no Billy.

"You think he crashed his bike because he was trying to avoid the poison ivy?" Becky asked.

"I don't know." The fear in Josh's stomach was growing. He thought about stopping to pray. But he wasn't sure what the others would think. They all went to church together, but they had never really prayed together on their own. They prayed in classes at the church building, and sometimes they prayed before soccer games, or when they went to do service projects, like cleaning yards or giving groceries to needy families. But an adult always started those prayers. Josh wanted to pray because he was afraid, but he wasn't sure how to do it and have the others join in. And besides that, he thought he would be embarrassed if they knew he was scared. So he just quietly said his own quick prayer.

"Hey, that looks like blood on the pedal!" Carlos yelled, pointing down at Billy's bicycle. The other kids got suddenly quiet. Carlos bent down to look more closely. "It's not a lot of blood, really, and I don't see any blood on the ground."

"There shouldn't be *any* blood, you guys," Josh groaned. The girls finally noticed that Josh was upset. Carlos was still looking at the bike pedal.

A dog barked nearby. Everyone looked up. The barking sound was coming from above them, almost as if a dog was in a tree. Then they saw a wagging tail in the thick brush and small trees high up on the side of the bluff.

"Molly!" Becky cried. "Here, Molly!"

The big golden retriever bounded down the side of the steep bluff.

"You'd think Molly would roll down, it's so steep," Josh said with surprise.

"Billy!" Emily yelled. There was no answer.

"You think he's hiding up there?" Carlos asked. "Maybe we should go look."

"Not me," Becky said. "I saw a snake on the top of that bluff last week when we were here. And it wasn't just a harmless garter snake. It was a great big, slimy, ugly snake that I'm sure had fangs. I think it could have been a rattlesnake."

"Snakes aren't really slimy," Carlos said.

"To me they are," Becky exclaimed.

"They may look slimy because they're shiny." Carlos was using his logical and precise voice. "Actually they're quite dry to the touch."

"I don't care if they're dry, shiny and smiling," Becky said. "Just keep them far away from me."

"Do you think Billy went looking for a snake?" Josh asked. "I wonder if he got bit. There are rattlesnakes still around. You guys stay here, and I'll go investigate."

Driven by worry and a sense of responsibility, Josh started climbing up the steep bluff. He turned to tell the others to stay together. They were all staring down the path, uneasy or even scared. Then Josh saw why. A man with dirty gray hair and a dirty gray beard was walking up the path toward them. He wore a red plaid shirt, old blue jeans and worn-out brown shoes. He stared straight at the children with intense blue eyes. As he came closer, Josh climbed back down to be near his friends. They all stepped off the path so the man could pass by. But the man stopped and stared at them. His face seemed made of stone.

"What you kids staring at?" the man asked. His voice was surprisingly deep and resonant.

"Nothing," Josh said, standing in front of the others.

"We just didn't expect to see anyone out here."

"This is a public park, ain't it?" the man demanded, more than asked.

"Yeah, sure it is," Josh said. "We're just looking for our friend. He left his bike here. We want to make sure he's okay."

"Your friend?" The man looked down at the ground and bike. Then he looked back at the children. "Better stay away from those weeds. That's poison ivy."

"We know." Julie smiled, but the strange looking man didn't smile back.

"Is your friend a little black kid about this high?" the man asked, holding his hand about four and a half feet off the ground.

"Yes, and he's my twin brother," Becky said eagerly. "Did you see him?"

"I think so," the man said slowly, pulling on his beard.

"Was he okay?" Josh asked.

"He was running pretty fast," the man said.

"Did he seem hurt?"

"I couldn't tell you that," the man said. "He was really moving. Looked to me like he was going to that clubhouse building over there by the lake." The man pointed across the park.

"Thanks, Mister," Josh said. "Let's go."

The children walked backward away from the grizzled, dirty man. He stared at them the whole time with his icy blue eyes.

"Be careful," the odd man said, his eyes wild. "You never know what trouble you might find, even in a pleasant park like this one."

He looked at each child one by one, seemed almost to smile, then walked down the path away from them. They watched him go in silence. Only when he was out of sight did anyone dare to speak.

"What a weirdo!" Carlos said. "That guy gives me the creeps in broad daylight."

"I think I've seen him before." Julie took off her glasses and rubbed the lenses slowly with her shirttail, trying to think.

"I've seen him too," Josh said.

"I know!" Julie said excitedly, putting her glasses back on. "He was with that group of homeless people down at the railroad bridge last Sunday. Remember when we took the sandwiches down there and invited them to the Luke Fourteen Party? I'm sure he was with them."

"He looks like a homeless person," Carlos said. The others nodded. The Luke Fourteen Party was an event their church was sponsoring for the poor and homeless people in Springdale.

"He looks like he's from outer space to me," Becky added. "Did you see those eyes? I've never seen such strange eyes before. He just stared and stared like he was looking right through you."

"Well, he's gone," Josh said. "Let's go check out the clubhouse. We need to make sure Billy is okay."

"What about our bikes and leaf samples?" Carlos asked.

"We can pick them up after we find Billy," Josh said.

"No one will bother them. Let's go."

As the children ran for the clubhouse, they didn't notice the tall stranger with the gray hair and red plaid shirt standing at the top of the bluff. As he watched the children, a crooked smile slowly spread across his face.

Chapter Two

The Golden Cup

Billy, where have you been?" Becky yelled when she saw her brother.

Billy was talking to a woman sitting in a station wagon. He stepped back as the car drove away. "I was talking to Mrs. Plutarch." Mrs. Plutarch was a member of their church. She had taught the first-grade Sunday-school class for several years.

"It looked like you rode your bike down the side of the bluff and crashed by the oak tree," Josh said with concern.

"Yeah, I did." Billy gave a big, proud smile.

"You're kidding!" Becky said. "Mom and Dad won't be happy when they hear about that. First you forget to wear your bike helmet today, and then you go shooting down that bluff. You could have hurt yourself."

"I did hurt myself," Billy replied. "But it was just a scrape."

He held up his arm which had a large scrape near his elbow. Then he showed them his leg which was also scraped below the right knee.

"We saw blood on one of the pedals." Carlos leaned forward to examine Billy's wounds.

"I'm okay." Billy could tell by the frown on Josh's face that the older boy had been worried. "Besides, if I hadn't gone down the bluff, I might not have found the cup."

"What cup?" Becky asked.

Billy took a bright golden cup out his leaf sample bag. All the children stared with surprise.

"It's the kind of cup that belongs in a tea service," Julie said. "My grandmother has a set like that, only hers is made of silver. That's an expensive cup. Where did you get it?"

"By the oak tree," Billy said. "It was just lying in the dirt. I came over here to see if anyone knows who it belongs to."

"Do they?" Julie asked.

"Mrs. Plutarch didn't know, but she thought I should ask people inside the clubhouse." Billy sprinted for the door.

"Nothing slows him down." Josh felt relieved that his friend was okay. He felt embarrassed that he had been afraid and that the others had probably noticed his fear back at the tree. "We'd better go make sure he doesn't cause any more trouble."

Since it was Seniors' Game Day, the Lakeside Club was filled with about two dozen senior citizens playing bridge, rummy, dominoes and other games. There were four people at each card table. The children knew some of the people since they were members of the Springdale Community Church where the children attended. Billy took the cup over to Mrs. Witherspoon.

"That's an expensive item, no doubt about it," Mrs. Witherspoon said with an air of authority. She was head of the Springdale Beautification League. "That's not just cheap gold plate either. That cup belongs to an expensive service. I bet it's genuine Cartright or Le Stradt."

"There's writing on the bottom," Billy said.

Mrs. Witherspoon turned the cup over. She squinted through her bifocals, holding the cup a little bit farther away as she read.

"There is writing," she murmured.

"It says 'George W. Baniston,' " Billy said.

" 'George W. Baniston,' " the woman read slowly.

"That's what I said," Billy said impatiently.

"How in the world would you come up with a cup that belongs to the Baniston family?" Mrs. Witherspoon asked. "They were the richest family in Springdale until Ingrid Baniston died. But that was ten years ago. I went to the estate auction. I don't remember seeing a tea service like this one at the auction, though."

"I didn't see anything like it either," said Mrs. Petticoat, a short, plump woman whose white hair had a purplish tinge. "I was at the auction. Remember? I bought that beautiful walnut roll-top desk."

"How could any of us forget that, dear?" Mrs. Witherspoon asked with a note of irritation in her voice. "You only bid against my husband the whole evening for the things I wanted—especially that desk."

"Now, now, ladies," said Mr. Harcourt, a tall, thin man with thick white hair. "That was ten years ago. Let's see this cup."

Mr. Harcourt held the cup in his hand and turned it over. He too read the inscription on the bottom. "Very strange, very strange indeed. Has anyone ever seen this cup before? It seems to have belonged to the George Baniston family."

Mr. Harcourt held up the cup. He passed the cup to the first table of bridge players. The cup passed from hand to hand. Billy and the other kids looked at each other.

"I bet it's really valuable," Billy said.

"Of course it's valuable, child," Mrs. Witherspoon said. "George Baniston was the richest man around here. He wouldn't buy a cheap tea service. That man had class. And wonderful taste in furniture. Especially in roll-top desks." She glanced sideways at Mrs. Petticoat, who merely smiled smugly.

"Now ladies, let's not quibble over bygones," Mr. Harcourt said.

A small, thin man carried the cup carefully back up to the children. His mouth was turned down and sour, as if he'd been sucking on a lemon for half a day. "Who found this cup?"

"I did," Billy said softly.

"Stole it more likely," Mr. Craven scowled.

"I did not steal it. I found it."

"Where?"

"Out in the park."

"Sounds like a made-up story to me," Mr. Craven said. "Why aren't you kids in school? This isn't a holiday."

"We are in school," Josh explained. "All of us are in home school, and we were out collecting leaf samples for our science class when Billy found the cup."

"Home schoolers, eh," Mr. Harcourt said. "I read an article in the paper about you kids. Sounds like a good way to learn. The whole world is your classroom. You can be learning all the time."

"I like it," Josh said with a smile. "We have more free time because we're usually able to get our work done more quickly than kids in regular school."

"I still think kids should be in a school where you can keep an eye on them," Mr. Craven grunted. "Keep them out of trouble."

"Kids can make plenty of trouble in school, believe me," said Mr. Harcourt said, a retired high-school principal. "I've got friends teaching in schools with policemen and security guards in the hallways just to keep order. Schools aren't what they used to be when you and I were kids, Mr. Craven."

"Kids aren't like what they used to be either," the old man said, glaring at Billy.

"These are wonderful children, Mr. Craven," Mrs.

Petticoat said. "Don't you know they are the ones who helped my mother clean up her yard and paint her porch? Josh and all these children helped her all day Saturday a few weeks ago. They worked hard and did a wonderful job. Not only that, they wouldn't take a dime for their efforts. They were real servants, just like Jesus."

"Servants, huh?" Mr. Craven said sourly. He still stared suspiciously at Billy and the golden cup.

"I know the perfect person to talk to about this cup," Mrs. Witherspoon said. "Mr. Finley at Finley's Antiques. He knew all about the Baniston family antiques. He bought a number of them at the estate sale. Maybe he knows who bought the tea service."

"He's the one, all right," Mrs. Petticoat added. "He knows more about antiques and jewelry than all of us combined."

"I don't know about that," Mr. Craven scoffed.

"Jasper Craven, you never have a good word to say about anyone," Mr. Harcourt said.

"I just don't think he's that knowledgeable," the small, thin man grunted. "I wanted to sell him an antique necklace that belonged to my mother, and he would only give me a quarter of what it was really worth. The man is crooked, I think. And cheap. He's always been that way."

"I've always found him very fair," Mrs. Witherspoon said to the children. "You just take this down to Finley's Antiques and see what he says. Do you know where his store is located?"

"Sure," Emily said. "I've been there before. He's the

one on Main Street in the old downtown. My mom bought a set of wooden chairs from him."

"She did?" Josh asked.

"The ones around the dining room table."

"Oh," Josh said. "Those old chairs."

"She thought she got a really good deal," Emily said.

"I'm sure she did." Mrs. Witherspoon looked at Mr. Craven. The old man grunted. He stared at the cup once more and then at the children. He looked as if he were about to say something else, but then stopped.

The children walked back to the bluff and got their bikes. As they got ready to leave, Josh suddenly stopped. At the far end of the cemetery, he saw a familiar looking red plaid shirt. The strange man with the gray beard was leaning against a tree and looking their way.

"I think someone is watching us," Josh whispered excitedly.

"What do you mean?" Billy asked, looking over at the man.

"We were talking to that guy earlier," Carlos said. "He's one of those homeless folks who hangs out by the railroad bridge. He's kind of creepy, I think."

"He hasn't done anything wrong, really," Julie said.

"Well, he looks creepy and acts creepy to me," Carlos replied, staring across the cemetery. "I don't trust him. Why's he watching us?"

"I don't know." Josh looked at the man. "Let's just get out of here and go to Mr. Finley's. That man won't bother us if we all stick together."

The other children nodded. Everyone but Billy put

on a bike helmet. In a moment they were riding on the narrow asphalt road that led out to the cemetery gate. As they passed through the iron gate, Josh looked over his shoulder. The man with the piercing blue eyes was still watching.

Mr. Finley's Antiques

The six children raced on their bicycles toward the old downtown section of Springdale. As in a lot of small towns, the original old brick buildings of Springdale had undergone many changes. Most of the original stores had closed years ago as shopping malls took away business. But in the last ten years the old downtown of Springdale had been revitalized. There was a bakery and a coffee shop and three different restaurants. Benson's Hardware was still open, as were the old drugstore and music store. The old Woolworth store had closed, but the Springdale Toystore was still in business.

Finley's Antiques was at the corner of Main and Tenth Street. As usual, Billy rode a little faster than the others and was the first one into the quaint store. The other children were right behind him. A bell on the door jingled. The inside of the store was a little dark, and everyone stood still for a moment.

"Smells funny in here." Billy sniffed the air.

"It's kind of musty," Emily replied.

The place was absolutely packed with all kinds of things, from rocking chairs and wooden desks to glass vases and lamps. On one side of the store were old wood and glass display cases with jewelry and old coins in view. A shelf above the case held old toy cars, trucks and tractors. A long shelf of old dolls and books was on the opposite wall.

"Look at all this stuff," Billy said. "He's got more junk than I've ever seen before."

"Shhhshssshhhh!" Julie whispered. "These are antiques, not junk."

"What about those old wooden tennis rackets?" Billy pointed above the door. "If you hit a ball with those, they'd break into a million pieces."

"Can I help you children?" a man called out. The children looked down the narrow aisle that led to the back of the store. A smiling man with white hair walked toward them. Becky giggled and Josh's mouth dropped open. The man was wearing ridiculous clothes—a big polka dot shirt with an orange tie, great big baggy purple pants and huge shoes.

"We . . . uh . . ." Billy started to say, but could only stare at the strangely dressed man.

"Haven't you kids ever seen a clown outfit before?" The old man pulled a bright orange wig out of the pocket of his pants and put it on his head. Then he took a bright red ball and slipped it over his nose.

"You *are* a clown!" Becky giggled.

"Not quite yet. I was just about to put on my makeup, but I'm late. I'll need to put it on at the party. I've got a grandson turning three, and I'm the star attraction. You've been here before, haven't you?" The man in the clown outfit smiled as he looked at Emily.

"My mom bought a set of oak chairs for our dining room last fall." Emily was impressed that he remembered her.

"Oh, yes. Mrs. Morgan. I rarely forget a customer. Now how can I help you?"

"We found this cup, and Mrs. Witherspoon said you could maybe tell us about it." Billy held up the cup.

Mr. Finley took the cup carefully. "Nice piece. Genuine Le Stradt, I'd say. Finest they made."

"There's writing on the bottom," Josh said.

Mr. Finley turned the cup over. As he read the writing, his expression suddenly changed. He pulled off his funny wig and red nose. He frowned and looked at the cup more closely. Without saying a word, he turned and walked over to an old desk covered with piles of papers and magazines. He opened a drawer and took out a magnifying glass. He looked at the writing on the bottom of the cup more closely. He sat down slowly in the desk chair.

"It can't be . . ." he whispered. "Not after all these years . . ."

"Can't be what?" Josh asked.

"Where did you get this?" Mr. Finley asked Billy.

"I found it by the big oak tree under the bluff down in the park by the lake."

"The big oak tree?" the man asked. "Are you sure?"

Just then the telephone rang. Mr. Finley picked it up. "Yes, yes, I know I'm late. I'll be right over."

"Do you know something about this cup?" Josh asked.

"I certainly do. Does anyone else know about it?"

"We showed it to the people playing cards in the Lakeside Clubhouse today," Emily said.

"They knew about George W. Baniston," Josh said.

"But they didn't recognize this piece?" Mr. Finley asked in surprise.

"They said to bring it to you, so here we are," Billy replied. "They said you might know who bought this from the Baniston family."

"There's a very interesting story behind this cup." Mr. Finley looked at his watch. "But I don't have time to tell you today since I'm already late for my party. With your permission I'd like to keep this cup in my safe overnight. We also need to let Sheriff Weaver hear about this. But first tell me all your names."

After introductions Josh asked, "Do you know who the cup belongs to?"

"Yes and no," the old man said mysteriously. "It's a long story, though, and I'm late. Could you come back at eight in the morning? This is a very valuable piece in more ways than one. That's why I'd like your permission to keep it in my safe."

"Well, it doesn't really belong to me," Billy said. "I just

found it. I would like to know what you're talking about."

"Me too," Josh said quickly. The others agreed.

The old man took the cup into his crowded office and put it in an old safe. He smiled and led the children to the front of the store. He locked the front door. "Be here at eight o'clock in the morning. And to be on the safe side, I would advise you not to say anything about this cup to anyone else until we talk to Sheriff Weaver. Of course you can tell your parents, but I mean people you don't know extremely well. Don't tell anyone where you found it, do you understand?"

The children all nodded. They were surprised at the urgent tone in his voice. Mr. Finley climbed into his maroon station wagon and waved as he drove away. The children stood on the sidewalk by their bikes.

Down the street, a pair of binoculars was trained on the children, but none of them sensed they were being spied on.

"What do you suppose he knows?" Julie asked.

"I think we may have stumbled onto a real mystery here," Josh said. "But what could it be?"

"Mr. Finley sure acted like it was something more than just an ordinary cup," Emily said.

"Well, it is a *gold* cup," Billy said. "And I found it. Wait until I tell Mom and Dad. Maybe there will be some kind of reward."

"That's possible," Josh said. "Mr. Finley certainly knows something about the cup that he hasn't told us so far."

Just as Mr. Finley drove away in his old van, Josh saw someone. He was standing two blocks away, leaning against a telephone booth by the Springdale Christian Bookstore. "We've got company," Josh said softly to the others.

"What do you mean?" Carlos asked.

"Down by the bookstore." Everyone looked. The man with the red plaid shirt seemed to look at the children and then turned away.

"Do you think he's following us?" Billy asked excitedly. "Just let him try and do anything. I'll crash right into him with my bike."

"He's just standing there, Billy," Julie chided. "He's probably lonely."

"I wish he'd be lonely somewhere else," Emily said. "It seems like he's following us."

"Let's just leave," Josh said. He suddenly felt afraid again. He hoped the others did not notice it. "We just have to stick together. Everyone check into the computer tonight, and we'll decide what to do about tomorrow."

"Right," Billy said.

"Let's all ride together till we get to Maple Street," Josh said. The other children nodded. In a few moments they were all heading down the road toward home.

All the way Josh was wondering about the rare gold cup and the things Mr. Finley said. He also thought about the strange man in the plaid shirt. He was halfway home when Josh remembered to thank God for answering his silent prayer by the oak tree about finding Billy.

As he thought about the gold cup, he realized there was something new to pray about.

Josh and Emily pedaled up their driveway and parked their bicycles in the garage. They carried the bags of leaf samples inside and set them on the workbench.

"I'm going to check in on the Net," Emily said. "I can't wait to e-mail some of my friends about Billy's discovery. Wait till they find out that we're involved in a real mystery."

"Yeah, but don't forget what Mr. Finley said. You better not tell anyone else until he's had a chance to talk to the sheriff."

"You're right," Emily said disappointedly. Emily loved everything electronic. She was the first one in the family to get her ham radio license, and she used her computer twice as much as anyone else. She had convinced Josh and her mom to get their ham radio licenses too. Josh liked the ham radio and used the computer on some of his home school work, but he wasn't as devoted a user as his sister.

Most of the home schooled kids in Springdale had access to a computer. Many families had their own, and those who didn't usually got to use someone else's computer in the home school co-op. As an engineering professor at the university, Mr. Morgan used computers all the time. There had always been a computer in their home as far back as Josh could remember. When home school supply companies started offering lessons using computer software, Josh's family was one of the first in the area to try out the new programs. The Morgans had even been asked to test some of the educational CD-ROM software created for home schoolers. So far, he and Emily liked most of the packages they had been able to use. They were supposed to use them for another three months and send in their reports to the software companies.

Besides using educational software, Emily liked using the computer to communicate with her friends on the local electronic bulletin board. Mr. Walden, their music tutor, had originally set up a bulletin board for the churches in the community. As a retired university professor, Mr. Walden took a lot of joy in setting up what he called the Kingdom Net.

The Kingdom Net was a bulletin board available to all the churches in the area around Springdale. Through the bulletin board, churches shared needs, news and electronic mail. There was even an on-line library of Bible reference materials that people could access. Mr. Walden was able to send out and receive electronic mail, bulletins and files from other parts of the country by using an Internet service. More and more Christians used the Kingdom Net as the local churches realized its value as a communication service.

Emily especially liked writing e-mail, or electronic letters, to her friends and relatives. The Morgans had cousins who home schooled in Oregon. Emily wrote to Sally, who was her age, at least once a week. While Emily was typing away at the computer, Josh went into the kitchen.

"Did you get your leaf samples?" Mrs. Morgan kept slicing potatoes.

"Yeah, and you won't guess what happened!" Josh said excitedly.

"You can tell me while you set the table. It's your turn to make biscuits tonight too. We're having pot roast."

Josh nodded. As he quickly set the table he told his mother about Billy disappearing, finding him and then the golden cup.

"And Mr. Finley really acted funny when he saw the cup," Josh said. "He even locked it in his safe. He wants to talk to us tomorrow. And he wants to tell Sheriff Weaver too."

"How odd," Mrs. Morgan said.

"Did you tell her about that creepy old guy who was watching us?" Emily asked as she walked into the room. "Julie thinks she saw him down at the railroad bridge. He was with the homeless people we gave sandwiches to last Sunday afternoon when we invited them to the Luke Fourteen Party."

"Don't be too quick to judge people, especially poor people, by their appearance," Mrs. Morgan said. "Isn't that what Pastor Brown has been teaching us?"

"But this guy was really creepy, Mom," Josh said.

"I'm not saying that you shouldn't be careful around strangers," Mrs. Morgan said. "But did this man actually do anything dangerous or threatening?"

"I guess not," Josh said slowly.

"He did tell us where we could find Billy," Emily added.

"God means for us to be wise about people." Mrs. Morgan started tossing the salad. "But it's not fair to jump to conclusions about people without knowing them."

"I guess not," Emily said.

The phone rang. Josh picked it up. He talked for a while. When he hung up, he let out a whoop. "That was Billy, and guess what happened? Some stranger called him and demanded to know where Billy found the cup. When Billy asked his name, the person refused to answer. Billy got suspicious and wouldn't tell him where he found the cup. He told the person he was going to talk to Mr. Finley and Sheriff Weaver about it in the morning. Then he told the caller to talk to the sheriff if he wanted more information."

"Then what happened?" Emily asked.

"Nothing," Josh said. "The caller just hung up."

Chapter Four

The
Blue
Van

The next day, Billy and Carlos met at Josh's house. Josh quickly put on his bike helmet and joined his friends. All three boys headed out on their bicycles toward the store. Josh took his two-meter ham radio and promised to call Emily as soon as Mr. Finley told them what he knew about the cup. Emily had agreed to teach Becky and Julie how to use a new geography program that morning.

"I didn't sleep too well last night because I kept thinking about that golden cup," Billy said. "I think it's really valuable."

"But it's just one cup." Josh didn't want Billy to get too excited.

"Maybe we should go back over by the tree and look around and see if there's more to be found," Billy said. "I bet we could find all sorts of stuff. Come on. Let's just go for a quick peek, and then go to the antique store."

"We need to stick to our plan," Josh said, trying to calm Billy down. When Billy got excited, he did crazy things. Josh didn't want Billy leading them on a wild goose chase. "We told Mr. Finley we'd be there at eight o'clock, and we'll be late if we go clear out to the park now."

"But what if there's more treasure?" Billy demanded.

"It will still be there," Josh said. "After all, no one except us and Mr. Finley knows exactly where you found the cup. Besides, that place is covered with poison ivy."

"I know," Billy said. "I woke up with terrible itching this morning. It's on my leg and on my arm." Billy let go of his right handlebar to show his arm. Angry bumps were all up and down his forearm where Billy had been scratching.

"If we go poking around in that stuff anymore, we'll all be itching to death," Josh said. "Let's just hear what Mr. Finley has to say first."

"Okay," Billy agreed reluctantly. "But I hope we don't miss our chance to dig up something wonderful."

They rode in silence into the old part of Springdale. As they passed the alley behind Main Street, Josh glanced over and saw a blue van behind Mr. Finley's store. Just then, Mr. Finley stumbled into the alley from his back door. Someone wearing a green ski mask was right behind Mr. Finley, his hand at Mr. Finley's back. That was all Josh saw as he rode past the alley entrance.

He hit the brakes on his bicycle hard. The other boys stopped too.

"Something's wrong!" Josh whispered harshly. "I think Mr. Finley's in trouble."

"What?" Billy asked.

"I just saw him get pushed out of his own store by a guy wearing a mask. I think he had a gun pointed at Mr. Finley's back."

"You're kidding, right?" Carlos asked with a smile.

Josh shook his head. He laid his bicycle on the side of the road by the sidewalk and quickly crept back over to the alley. Billy and Carlos were right behind him. All they saw was the blue van. Then it started up. It moved slowly down the alley away from them.

"Mr. Finley's in there," Josh said.

"Are you sure?"

"I'm positive," Josh said.

"You saw a gun?" Billy asked, his voice rising.

"I think so. It all happened so fast and then they were out of sight," Josh said. "What should we do?"

"Follow it!" Billy said. He ran back for his bicycle and hopped on it. Without hesitating, he pedaled down the alley. In a moment, the smaller boy was chasing after the old blue van.

"Billy, are you crazy? Come back!" Josh yelled. But their smaller friend showed no sign of slowing down.

"We have to go," Josh yelled. Both boys ran for their bikes. By the time they reached the alley, Billy was almost half a block ahead of them. At the end of the alley, the blue van turned left on Grand Avenue.

The speed limit in town was only thirty miles an hour and the van was going even slower. Josh and Carlos headed down Grand Avenue. Billy was still ahead of them by at least a block.

"Billy's really moving," Josh yelled.

Carlos nodded, taking deep gulps of air as he pedaled even faster. Even though they were going as fast as they could, the van was pulling away from them.

At Morrison Street, the van stopped for a light. The boys all gained ground. When the light turned green, they were only two blocks behind. They made the green light and turned quickly onto Morrison just as the van turned onto Old Highway 17.

"He might be heading out of town," Josh panted. "We'll never catch him once he does. I'll call Emmy at the house. Maybe she can follow them."

Josh pulled his two-meter radio out of his backpack. He slowed down enough to steer with one hand while holding the radio with the other.

"WA5XNZ, this is WA5XCN, do you read me?" Josh said into the radio. "Josh to base. Josh to base. Are you there, Emmy?"

A few seconds later, the radio crackled to life. "This is base, WA5XNZ," Emily's voice crackled over the radio. "What's up, Josh?"

"Not much time to talk," Josh said. "Get on your bike and go out to Highway 17 by the railroad. Watch for an old blue van and follow it as far as you can. Over."

"What's going on?" Emily asked.

"Just do it," Josh shouted. "We think someone has

kidnapped Mr. Finley. We're following on our bikes now, but he's getting away. He's headed down Highway 17 now. If you hurry you might see the van. Please do it, Emmy. We're not kidding around."

"Okay, Josh. I'll take the other portable radio and let you know what I see. Julie and Becky will go with me. Over."

Josh left the radio on and stuck it in his jacket pocket. Far up the road, the van was pulling away. The road curved and went down a hill, and the van disappeared.

"Lord, keep all of us safe," Josh murmured as he pedaled faster. He hoped he was doing the right thing. He was concerned not only for Billy but for Mr. Finley. Up ahead, Billy was finally slowing down. Josh and Carlos caught up with their friend.

"He's getting away," Billy said angrily. "But I got his license plate number. Or at least part of it. KG6-79 something. There were two or three other numbers."

"Good work," Josh said. "We can tell it to the police. I radioed Emily to head out to Highway 17 and Belton Road. Maybe she can spot the van. We've got to help Mr. Finley if we can."

"Can you call the police on your radio?" Billy asked.

"Not on the two-meter band," Josh said. "They monitor CB's but not this kind of shortwave."

The three boys rode more slowly to catch their breath. They coasted down the curve in the road, riding single file. The radio inside Josh's backpack crackled to life.

"WA5XCN, this is WA5XNZ," a voice said.

"It's Emily." Josh took out the radio. "This is

WA5XCN. What's up, Emily?"

"We're on Belton Road heading to Highway 17. You may be in luck. I see the tail end of a train up ahead. He may have had to wait at the crossing at Highway 17."

"I hope so," Josh answered. "Just try to keep the van in sight as long as you can. We're going on Highway 17 now heading your way. Let me know if you see anything, over."

"Will do, over." Emily, Julie and Becky pedaled as fast as they could go. Becky was out in the lead. As she started down a hill she shouted out, "I see it! There's a van at the railroad crossing."

Emily held the radio up to her mouth as she went down the hill. The van was stopped, but the caboose of the train had just crossed Highway 17. The long, wooden crossing guard lifted slowly into the air and the van began moving.

"The van's going again," Emily said into the radio.

"Keep it in sight as long as possible," Josh said. "And tell us if you see anything."

"We're almost to Highway 17 now," Emily said. The girls slowed down only slightly as they turned onto the highway. The van was already a quarter mile down the road ahead of them. They pedaled single file and sped up.

"We'll never keep up," Julie yelled to Emily who was in the lead. She pedaled faster, but it seemed useless. The van was getting smaller and smaller. The road was long and flat. The three girls kept pedaling hard.

"Look, it's turning," Becky shouted. She pointed.

The van was over a mile away. It turned left, then disappeared from their view.

Emily picked up the radio. "The van is out of sight. We saw it turn left onto some road about a mile ahead of us."

"I copy you," Josh said. "Wait for us there. We should be there in about five minutes."

"We're just beyond the railroad crossing on Highway 17." The other girls slowed down since they could hear Josh too.

"It can't be a big road where the van turned off," Becky said.

"No, it's not," Emily replied. "The next big road is over that hill about a half mile."

A few minutes later, Josh, Billy and Carlos passed over the railroad crossing and coasted to a stop by the girls.

"He turned about a mile down the road." Emily pointed. "But it can't be a big road. Maybe he didn't go too far. Are you sure Mr. Finley was in there?"

Josh quickly recounted what he had seen. "I don't know for sure that this guy had a gun, but he wore a green ski mask. And I'm sure the other person was Mr. Finley."

"Could it have been a woman in the ski mask?" Julie asked.

"I suppose it could have," Josh said. "I just assumed it was a man. It all happened so fast. I think we should go check it out. It's not much more than a mile down there. If we don't see anything, we can come back. But if there's a trail of some kind, I think we should follow it while it's fresh."

"I want to go," Billy chimed in.

"Me too," said Julie. The other children started pedaling down the road.

As usual, Billy ripped out in front on his smaller bike, but after a few minutes he began to run out of wind and slowed down. The other children caught up with him. Together, they headed two by two down the lonely road. Only one car passed them as it went into Springdale. They pedaled on steadily.

"He must have turned up there," Emily shouted, pointing to a small dirt road that led off Highway 17. The riders all turned onto the road which led back into the woods. A set of fresh tire tracks was clearly visible in the dirt. Billy shot out ahead down the dirt road. The other kids looked at each other.

"We've come this far," Josh said. "We might as well keep going. Besides, we'll have to keep Billy out of trouble."

They followed their friend down the bumpy dirt road. For a moment, he disappeared as the road curved into the forest. Emily slowed down. "This is getting sort of scary."

"I know," Carlos replied.

"What if we—"

"I see something!" Billy shouted.

"Shhhssshhhhh!" Josh commanded. Billy sped up and disappeared around another curve in the road. Josh frowned and sped up. As soon as he rounded the curve, he hit the brakes and swerved to avoid hitting Billy, who had stopped in the middle of the dirt road. At the same time, he saw what Billy was staring at. Down a winding driveway, out in a weedy, overgrown yard was an abandoned farmhouse. The blue van was parked in the weeds by the back of the house.

All the other bike riders came to a sudden halt beside Billy and Josh. They looked at the van quietly.

"Now what?" Emily asked. "I guess we caught it."

"We go check it out," Billy said eagerly.

"But what if this person did have a gun?" Emily asked Josh. "You can't let Billy go up there. This could really be dangerous, Josh."

Josh nodded slowly, never taking his eyes off the van. He wasn't sure what to do. Cold fear gripped his belly. Everything had happened so fast, but now the danger of the situation was sinking in. Once again he wanted to pray, but for some reason he felt tongue-tied and intimidated by his fears.

"Lord, help us, please!" Josh muttered quickly. The other children paused when they realized Josh was praying. The older boy stopped, his eyes lighting up with an idea.

"Josh to base, Josh to base, come in base," Josh said. He waited a few seconds and repeated the call.

"Mom was outside in the garden when we left," Emily said. "But I didn't leave a note since you told us to hurry."

"Josh to base, Josh to base, come in base?" Josh said. He waited a few seconds and repeated the call. This time the radio crackled in response.

"This is your mother, Josh," a woman's voice said over the radio. "What's up and where is everyone? All the girls are gone."

"They're with Carlos and Billy and me. We're okay, but we have a strange situation here. Over."

"What do you mean?" Mrs. Morgan asked.

Josh told her everything that had happened up until that moment as quickly as possible.

"We can see the van now, but we don't see anyone else," Josh said. "Please call the police and have them come out here right away."

"I will. But I want you kids to get out of there right now," commanded his mother. "Wait out on Highway 17 so the police can see you."

"Okay," Josh said. "We're leaving now. Over."

"Be careful," Mrs. Morgan said. "I'm signing off."

"We need to wait by the—"

"Help! Help!" a man's voice called out from the direction of the house.

Billy jumped off his bicycle and ran for the house.

"Billy, come back!" Becky yelled. But her brother didn't slow down.

"Josh, do something!" Becky said frantically. "You've got to stop Billy."

"You all go out to the road like Mom said," Josh replied. "Go now. I'll go after Billy."

He took a deep breath and began to run, praying every step of the way.

Chapter Five

Robbed!

Josh ran as fast as he could after his friend, but moving through the tall weeds and fallen branches wasn't easy. He tripped several times before he slowed down.

"Help! Help!" a man's voice yelled again. By the time Josh caught up to Billy, both boys were at the corner of the rickety, old porch of the house. Billy moved down the side of the house toward a window where the glass was broken out.

"Help!" the voice called. The voice was coming from inside the house.

"Billy, come back!" Josh whispered loudly.

Without answering, Billy slowly peeked up through the window. He looked excitedly at Josh and waved him forward. Josh frowned, but tiptoed along the side of the house to the window.

"Look!" Billy said so softly Josh could barely hear. Josh's heart was beating hard. He raised up his head and looked through the window.

In the middle of a large room, a man with white hair was tied to a chair. The chair had tipped over on the floor with the man's back to them. Josh looked carefully around the room. No one else was there.

Without a word, Josh jumped and pulled himself up through the window. His heart was pounding as he crossed the floor. He had his pocketknife out by the time he reached the man. "I'll cut the ropes," Josh whispered.

The man turned his head. A large bandanna covered half of Mr. Finley's mouth. Josh carefully cut the heavy rope that bound the man to the old wooden chair.

"Where did you come from?" the old man said with surprise. He sat up, rubbing his wrists and arms in pain.

"We better get out of here," Josh whispered.

"He's gone." Mr. Finley struggled to his feet. "Anyway, I *think* he's gone."

"But the blue van is outside."

"He left in another vehicle," the old man said. "I know it wasn't the van because the motor sounded different. He must have left about ten minutes ago."

"Who was it?" Josh asked.

"I don't know." Mr. Finley brushed off his trousers. "He wore a ski mask and had a gun. He was waiting in my store this morning. Once we got in the van, he covered my head with that bag. It fell off when I tipped the chair over." Mr. Finley picked up a large paper grocery bag off the floor.

"Are you all right?" Billy yelled from outside the window.

"We better go out to the road," Josh said. "We contacted my mom by ham radio and she was going to call the police."

"They'll certainly want to hear about this." Mr. Finley shook his head. "All this happened because of that golden cup that friend of yours found yesterday."

Mr. Finley and Josh found their way out of the old, abandoned house. On the other side of the house there was another driveway. Fresh car tracks matted down the grass and weeds. Mr. Finley looked at the house carefully.

"This is the old Garner farm," Mr. Finley said. "No one has lived out here for years. How did you know I was here?"

Josh quickly explained how they got to the house. Mr. Finley smiled in amazement.

"I'm going to go tell the others we found Mr. Finley," Billy yelled, running for his bike.

"He really gets around," Mr. Finley observed with a smile.

"I wasn't sure what to do when Billy ran up here," Josh said. "I was afraid that you might be hurt and that Billy would get hurt."

"Well, I sure started praying as soon as I saw that gun back in my shop." Mr. Finley winked. "I don't mind telling you I was plenty scared. You kids did a brave thing coming after me like that."

"I was really scared too," Josh said softly. The old man smiled and patted Josh on the back.

"I owe a lot to you and Billy and the other kids. You all are quite a team."

As they walked around to the rear of the house, the sheriff's car roared to a stop out on the dirt road. The sheriff got out of the car with his gun drawn.

"Everything's okay now, Bob, thanks to these young detectives!" Mr. Finley yelled out.

A few minutes later the other children and Mrs. Morgan arrived at the old house.

"What's this all about?" Sheriff Weaver asked, his face lined with concern. "Was it a robbery?"

"Oh, yes, it was a robbery all right," Mr. Finley said. "But only an old golden cup from a tea service was taken."

"The cup I found?" Billy asked in dismay.

"I'm afraid so," the old man replied, patting Billy on the shoulder. "I would have told you children the story yesterday, but I was in a hurry for my grandson's birthday party. I figured it could wait because that cup's been missing over thirty years."

"Thirty years?" Sheriff Weaver asked. "What's going on here, Mr. Finley?"

"This will take some time to explain," the old man said. "That gold cup Billy found was part of a mystery that's been haunting the town of Springdale for over thirty years. Most of you probably wouldn't remember it, except you might have heard old Sheriff Barns talk about it, Bob, since he was sheriff back then."

"What happened?"

"I don't remember the exact dates, but it was in the fall, like now, when there was a robbery in Springdale,"

Mr. Finley said. "It wasn't your ordinary robbery. Several churches and civic groups in the town back then took up a collection to build a shelter for old folks and people in need. They were going to call it the Springdale Shelter."

"Sort of like the Salvation Army?" Julie asked.

"Yes, a lot like that," Mr. Finley said. "The Springdale Community Church was leading the effort."

"The same church where our father is the pastor?" Julie asked.

"The same one," Mr. Finley replied. "Of course, that was back before you all even lived here. Anyway, as I said, several churches and civic groups were involved in this effort, as well as many citizens of Springdale. They called it the Springdale Shelter Project. They raised money in two ways. One was donations, and the other was a collection of valuables: jewels, coins, antiques and so on that were auctioned off. The cup that Billy found was part of a tea service donated by Mr. George M. Baniston."

"So it was auctioned off?" Josh asked.

"They never got to it," Mr. Finley said. "There were so many good donated items that they had to break the auction up into two nights. I remember it well. They held the first part of the auction on a Friday night down at city hall. They raised thousands of dollars, which was a lot of money back then. Anyway, as I said, there were so many items, they planned to auction the rest of the stamps and coins the next night. But that auction never took place, because of the robbery."

"What happened?" Carlos asked.

"Sometime around midnight on Friday, three thieves broke into city hall and looted the place. They took everything they could, including a large safe that had been holding all the money collected up until that time for the shelter project. Besides the money, there were very valuable coins and stamps in the safe, all donated by Mr. Baniston, who was at that time probably the wealthiest man in the county. No one knows for sure the value of the coins or stamps because the appraisers were going to come Saturday morning before the auction. I was part of the group that was to help determine their value, but I never got the chance."

"They took everything?"

"Everything they could carry off," Mr. Finley said. "Everybody in town was terribly upset. Lots of times a problem will bring people together, but the robbery just divided people and caused even more problems. Once the horse gets out of the barn, everyone has an opinion about what should have been done differently. Hindsight is always the easiest."

"Did they catch the thieves?" Josh asked.

"Yes and no," the old man said. "Because the building itself wasn't broken into, the police assumed it was an inside job. They arrested two janitors the next day and were hoping to arrest a third janitor, but he disappeared. Most people assume that the third man double-crossed his partners and made off with all the stolen goods. One janitor, I remember, insisted that he was totally innocent. The other janitor, who was actually caught with some of the stolen property, refused to answer any questions. They both went to jail. One man died a few years later in jail in some accident. The other man, the one who claimed he was innocent, served his time and got out. No one ever heard from him again. And no one found any of the stolen goods until yesterday when you found that cup," he said looking at Billy.

"You mean the case was never really solved?" Josh asked.

"Not according to Sheriff Barns," Sheriff Weaver said. "I remember him talking about this case. He always assumed that the third man got the money and escaped. But lots of people think the treasure may still be here somewhere."

"Mr. Baniston sent out a lot of bulletins describing the stolen coins and stamps to dealers all over the country," said Mr. Finley. "But he never heard any news."

"So you mean that the treasure might still be around?" Billy asked.

"Apparently at least one man thinks so." Mr. Finley rubbed his arm.

"The person who kidnapped you?" the sheriff asked.

"He was definitely interested in that cup and where it was found," Mr. Finley said. "That's what this was all about. He threatened to hurt me, so I told him what Billy said about finding it at the old oak tree. He took the cup with him."

"Could you identify this man?" the sheriff asked hopefully.

"If I could, we wouldn't be standing around talking

now," Mr. Finley said. "I never saw his face, and he was obviously disguising his voice. I say it was a man because he sounded like a man disguising his voice, if you know what I mean. But I didn't recognize it."

"But he must be someone from around here that you do know, or else he wouldn't have gone to the trouble to disguise his voice," Josh said excitedly.

"You're probably right about that," the sheriff said, looking at Josh with respect.

"I'd hate for it to be one of my own neighbors," Mr. Finley said. "I've lived in Springdale all my life and never had any problem with thieves except a few kids shoplifting. Riles me up to think someone can come and force me out of my own store. It's worse to think it may even be someone who knows me."

"But no one even knew you *had* that cup except us," Billy said.

"Those people at the clubhouse knew about the cup," Josh added. "And that weird-looking man."

"What man?" the sheriff asked.

"We think he's one of the homeless guys." Josh quickly told about the man they had first seen in the park.

"He saw us yesterday when we came out of Mr. Finley's antique store," Billy added. "He was hanging around acting real suspicious."

"I bet he's the one," Becky said. "Are you going to arrest him?"

"Hold on," the sheriff said. "I'll definitely talk to him, but it's too soon to be making accusations or arrests."

"You say Billy showed the cup to people at the clubhouse at the lake?"

"Yeah," Josh said. "There were lots of people there."

"Yesterday was their card party day." Sheriff Weaver nodded. "That's a lot of people."

"But we didn't talk to all of them," Billy said. "Just a few."

"But Mrs. Witherspoon said she would mention it to the others," Emily said. "The way she talks, I bet half the town knows Billy found that cup by now."

"Wait a minute!" Mr. Finley said. "This man asked where the cup was found. Why am I being so stupid? I told him where Billy said he found the cup."

"We didn't tell any of the people at the clubhouse where we found it," Billy said. "I just said I found it in the park."

"That's right," Julie said.

"I think we should all go to the park and take a look," the sheriff said. "And the sooner the better."

Ten minutes later, Mrs. Morgan parked her van at the Lakeside Clubhouse parking lot. Everyone scrambled to get out. Billy led the way to the bluff, followed by the sheriff, Mr. Finley, Mrs. Morgan and all the children. Billy began to run when he got closer to the tree. He suddenly jumped up and down and shouted.

"Come on!" Billy yelled. Everyone hurried over. Billy stood by the big oak tree. Every one was quiet for a moment as they looked down. Near the base of the tree, almost exactly where Billy had crashed, was a large, freshly dug hole.

Chapter Six

Detectives in the Making

L ooks like our kidnapper beat us here," the sheriff said. "But he didn't get to dig long enough to find anything. I wonder if he saw us coming and left."

"Then he could be nearby?" Billy asked.

"He's probably long gone by now," the sheriff said. "But he may come back, I reckon."

"Can you do a stakeout on this place?" Josh asked.

"We can keep checking, that's for sure," the sheriff said. "I can talk to some of the residents along the lake and ask them to keep their eyes open."

Just then, Mrs. Highsmith, a reporter for the *Springdale Gazette,* walked down the path with her camera in hand.

"Someone down at the police station called and said you had a story," the woman said.

"We do indeed," Sheriff Weaver said. "And these

children are the heroes. They may have saved Mr. Finley's life."

Sheriff Weaver explained about the golden cup. When he mentioned the part about Mr. Finley getting kidnapped, Mrs. Highsmith whistled. Mr. Finley told her what he knew about the Springdale Shelter robbery.

"This *is* a story," Mrs. Highsmith said. "I'm going to have to do some research back at the office."

"Research?" Josh asked with interest. "I'd like to know more about this case myself."

"Then why don't you come along," Mrs. Highsmith said. "After all, you all are part of the story now."

"May we go, Mom? Please?" Emily asked.

"I want to go too," Billy said. "Why should Josh and Emily have all the fun?"

"You can all come as far as I'm concerned," Mrs. Highsmith said. "I can show you how to use the microfilm viewer and how the newspaper keeps records. Of course the *Gazette* isn't as fancy as the big newspapers, but I can show you how we work."

Mrs. Morgan smiled at the eager faces. Mr. Finley laughed.

"Looks like you've got some detectives in the making, Sheriff," Mr. Finley said.

"I welcome all the help I can get," Sheriff Weaver said.

"It sounds like a learning experience to me," Mrs. Morgan said. "I'll take you there and call the other parents. We'll have to go back to the farm and get your bicycles later."

The children all cheered. Josh couldn't wait to start investigating.

Mrs. Highsmith took some photographs of the hole by the tree, and then a photograph of Billy, the other children and Mr. Finley by the tree.

Ten minutes later, they were all down at the *Springdale Gazette* office. Mrs. Highsmith led them around past the front desk and down into the basement.

"I usually start with the old newspaper stories," Mrs. Highsmith said. "I know Sheriff Barns was in charge back then and worked on this case. I'll need to talk to him. But first, I need to get as much background on the case as I can."

"So you know enough to ask the right questions," Josh said.

"That's right." The woman smiled. "You're talking like a detective now."

"It's sort of like a lot of our studies in home school," Josh said. "We do research on some subjects. That's why we were out by the bluff yesterday. We had been studying local plants and were trying to collect good specimens. We had studied enough to know sort of what we were looking at. Carlos has a whole library of Usborne books on science and other things. They're really fun to read."

"This place smells almost as good as the library." Julie grinned as she looked around the shelves and file cabinets. The other kids nodded. One thing they had in common was that they all liked books and magazines.

"We have bound copies of all the old issues here,"

Mrs. Highsmith said. "We also were able to put them on microfilm a few years ago. And if we needed to, we could go to the library at the university and look at some of the bigger national papers like the *New York Times, Los Angeles Times* and *Washington Post.*"

"I love the library at the university," Josh said. "Since my dad teaches there, we go there all the time. They have a lot more books than the Springdale Library."

Mrs. Highsmith moved her finger along the rows of bound volumes, then stopped and pulled one out. "This should be the right year."

"Let me look. Let me look," Billy said eagerly.

"That sounds like a good idea," Mrs. Highsmith said cheerfully. "Just turn the pages very carefully since they are so old. You and Josh and Julie can look here. And I'll show the other children the microfiche machine."

Billy, Josh and Julie crowded around the old book. Billy turned the pages one by one.

"Sheriff Weaver said it was in the fall," Julie said. "Skip ahead."

"Here it is!" Josh said excitedly. "And look. There's all kinds of pictures. This was front page news."

"Hey, there's a picture of a cup just like the one I found," Billy said.

"You mean there was another cup?"

"It looks just like the one I found," Billy said. "It had the same name on the bottom. And it was a key piece of evidence."

"Look at that!" Josh said, reading about the account. "That cup was found by the big oak tree near the bluff in Lakeside Park, according to Mr. Hastings, one of the accused men."

"How odd," Julie said. "Billy found the same kind of cup in the same place as a robbery that took place thirty years ago."

The children hurried to read the story about the robbery.

"We have it on the screen over here!" Carlos said. Mrs. Highsmith smiled. She read the story off the screen, jotting down a note every so often.

The children studied the papers and whispered. The newspapers covered the story through several issues, from the robbery through the trial. The children read every line of every story as if the robbery had just happened yesterday, rather than thirty years before.

"This is really something," Josh said. "I think we should write down all the facts in logical order as they came out in the trial."

"That's a good idea," Mrs. Highsmith said. "Meanwhile, I have to write my own story. You can work down here if you want. I use three-by-five index cards to gather facts and then arrange them in the correct order before writing it out on the computer or a legal pad."

She gave them a handful of blank cards and a yellow legal pad. Since Becky had the best handwriting, she was chosen to be the scribe. After an hour had whizzed by, the children had assembled a stack of cards and Becky had written out the story line of events on the yellow pad.

"What do we have so far?" Josh asked.

Becky cleared her voice and read out loud. "The auction on Friday night was over at 10:00 P.M. By 10:30 every one had left the city hall building, and it was securely locked up. The money from all the collections and the auction was locked up in a safe in a room at city hall. The tea service and other items not auctioned were left on a long table. The valuable coin collection and old stamps were locked in the safe.

"At 12:30 A.M., Mr. Robert Hastings said he was walking home from his cleaning job at the bakery. He said he saw the golden cup by the big oak tree near the bluff. He claimed he recognized the cup since he cleaned the courthouse building. He was curious and went back to the courthouse with the golden cup intending to see if it was misplaced. He said the side entrance door was open. He went inside. He heard a noise and went down the hall to the auction room. When he turned on the lights, he said he saw Clifford Smoot in the auction room carrying out a box of silverware. Clifford Smoot had his shirt off, and he was soaked with sweat, which was unusual since the fall weather was cool. Robert Hastings said that he noticed that most of the items and the safe were missing. Mr. Hastings was about to run and call the police, he said, when the police arrived. They had been cruising by, had seen the lights on and had come to investigate. They found the two janitors in the auction room arguing. They arrested them both.

"The police assumed there had to be a third man because the safe would have been too heavy for just two men. Since Mr. Arnold Baker, the third janitor, had disappeared without a trace, he was assumed to be the third thief. Mr. Hastings always claimed he was innocent, but no one believed him. The trial was fairly quick. Both men were sent to jail for ten years. After two years, Clifford Smoot died when he fell down some stairs in prison. We don't know what happened to Mr. Hastings, but we assume he got out of jail after he did his time. No one ever heard anything about Arnold Baker. And none of the stolen items ever turned up. Because of the theft, the Springdale Shelter to help out poor people was never built. Case closed."

"That's really sad," Julie said. "Just think of all the people that never got helped just because some mean thieves were greedy. Who were those guys anyway?"

"They were all sort of drifters, or homeless men. They lived in a place they called Shantytown outside of Springdale."

"I wonder where that is?" Billy asked.

"It must have been somewhere out beyond the park if Mr. Hastings said he was walking home," Josh said.

"But he was probably lying," Billy grunted.

"Maybe he wasn't," Julie said.

"Well, he went to jail for it," Billy said. "He must have been guilty."

"They were all very poor men and relatively new to town. Clifford Smoot and Arnold Baker were single men, but Robert Hastings had a twelve-year-old son and a ten-year-old daughter. He had three janitorial jobs, cleaning the courthouse, the bakery and the furniture factory."

"I read that Clifford Smoot did lots of odd jobs around town. He'd mow lawns, trim trees, dig graves and even clean out sewer lines—the kind of dirty jobs that no one wanted to do. He had lived in Dallas before coming to Springdale. In Dallas he had been in trouble for gambling and felony theft. He had stolen a car and had even gone to jail. No one knew he had a record when they hired him as a janitor."

"I bet they were sorry they hired him," Becky said, crinkling up her nose.

"The third man, Arnold Baker, was the one who disappeared. He had only been in town a month. Apparently Clifford Smoot had helped get him a job as a part-time janitor with the city. He had been arrested the night before for being drunk at work and lost his job. A few months after the trial they found out that he was wanted for murder in Louisiana. He had escaped from a small jail. He had been arrested but had escaped before the trial and had come to Springdale."

"You wouldn't think they would give keys to city hall to men like that," Josh said.

"They didn't," Emily said. "No one was sure how they did it, but they figured they stole a key and made a copy or something like that."

"That's sad," Julie said, looking down at the book of open newspapers.

"What?" Josh asked.

Julie pointed down at one of the newspaper stories. "There was a train accident a week before the robbery and two unknown men were killed out by the railroad bridge.

They didn't know their names, and no one even claimed their bodies."

"That is sad," Josh said. "But the robbery was much bigger news. Look at the size of the headlines."

Mrs. Highsmith came downstairs followed by Mr. Finley. The old man was beaming. Becky read their collection of events surrounding the robbery.

"That's real fine work," Mrs. Highsmith said.

"I agree," Mr. Finley added. "You kids have had a real busy morning, and I bet you're just as hungry for pizza as I am! Let's go before it gets too crowded."

"Pizza!" the children shouted. They rushed for the steps that led up to the door. Outside, the children scrambled into Mr. Finley's and Mrs. Highsmith's cars. As they rode away, a man sat in a car down the street, watching the children with binoculars. He dropped the binoculars on the front seat next to a green ski mask. Sticking out of the ski mask was the barrel of a black revolver. The man cursed softly and then followed the children to the pizza shop.

Chapter Seven

Buried
Treasure?

The next morning Josh and Emily came into the kitchen and saw the newspaper lying on the kitchen table. Josh smiled at the headlines.

"Home School Detectives Thwart Kidnapping!" blared across the top of the paper on page one. "Thirty-Year-Old Robbery Case Reopened," said the subhead.

The photograph showed all six children and Mr. Finley standing near the big oak tree by the freshly dug hole. "Is the Springdale Shelter treasure still hiding?" the caption below the photograph asked.

"Look at that!" Josh said. "We're on the front page of the newspaper." He read the beginning of the story out loud.

"Six brave children, riding bicycles and using two-meter ham radio receivers, rescued Springdale merchant Mr. George Finley when he was kidnapped during a robbery early Tuesday morning. The six home school children were out on a routine science study on Monday afternoon when they unknowingly opened up a thirty-year-old mystery. Billy Renner, age ten, found a golden cup from a tea service. They took the cup to a Springdale antique dealer, Mr. George Finley, for more information. Before Mr. Finley could confirm what the children had found, he was abducted from his shop early Tuesday morning by a masked gunman."

Josh read the rest of the article to himself. The story was so vivid, he began reliving the whole incident.

"It's a very nice article," Mrs. Morgan said. "Mrs. Highsmith is very thorough and fair. She said nice things about home schooling toward the end of the article too. She may do a follow-up article about the home school co-op. She interviewed your father and me. She was surprised that such a wide variety of people home school in this area. She was very impressed with your ability to research and your writing skills."

"We've done stuff like that before," Josh said. "It sort of reminded me of doing science experiments or research papers. Of course, this was different, but it does make you think and try to figure out what's going on. I really did feel like a detective."

"I wish we could solve the case and find out where the treasure is," Emily added as she read the article.

"This morning you need to be solving math, science, spelling and history before you go out trying to solve a robbery." Mrs. Morgan smiled. "I have your lessons ready. This evening you need to practice your music.

The Luke Fourteen Party is next Sunday, and Mr. Walden wants you to be ready to play."

"We'll be ready," Emily said. All six children had been playing instruments for the last two years. Josh played bass and guitar while Emily played the flute, Julie played the violin, Carlos played keyboards and piano, Becky played cello, and Billy, when he was allowed, played the drums. Mr. Walden made simple arrangements of classical compositions and some modern pieces. He was a good teacher but sometimes did get impatient with Billy and his drums. He almost always had to remind him to play more softly. On many of the pieces they were practicing for the Luke Fourteen Party, Billy wasn't going to play at all.

"Do you think there will be a lot of people at the Luke Fourteen Party?" Josh asked.

"Pastor Brown thinks there will be a good turnout," Mrs. Morgan said.

The Springdale Community Church called it a Luke Fourteen Party because it was inspired by a parable Jesus told in the New Testament book of Luke in the fourteenth chapter starting at the sixteenth verse. Pastor Brown and many leaders in the church had a desire to help people in Springdale who were usually ignored and overlooked because of poverty and other problems.

One of the ways the church was trying to do this was by having the party. Many of the church members had invited homeless and needy families from the community to come. There would be games for the children, musical presentations and a time of worship. Each church member was to provide transportation for those they invited if the guests didn't have a way to get to the party. The church would also give out clothing and groceries.

"I had almost forgotten about the party since Billy found that cup," Josh said. "We're still taking the Carson family, aren't we?"

"Sure we are," Emily said. Mrs. Carson was a single mother with three preschool children who lived in an old bus out by the railroad bridge.

"Good," Josh said. "You know, I didn't think I'd like doing the servant projects at first. I thought the work would be boring or too hard. But it's turned out to be exciting."

"Helping people makes me feel useful," Emily said. "Before, we just went to class. Now we go out and do stuff that's important."

"I think that's what makes it exciting," Josh said. "I never knew what people were talking about when they said the love of God was working through them. But now I think I do, and it's neat."

"Pastor Brown takes young people seriously," Mrs. Morgan said. "All Christians, including young Christians, have gifts and talents that God means for us to use in the church and the community."

"Show and Tell." Josh was quoting a phrase Pastor Brown used often. "Show people God's love and tell them about Jesus."

Through Pastor Brown's help and encouragement, the young people in the church had begun spending time with older people or others who needed help in Springdale. They did yardwork, housework, car washing, gardening and all sorts of things. One Saturday they picked up trash along the roads. Another time they helped clean and fix up a rundown playground near an apartment complex. Almost all the young people in the church were involved.

The phone rang. Mrs. Morgan picked it up. She listened for a moment and then hung up.

"That was Nancy at the sheriff's office," Mrs. Morgan said. "There's been a new development in the case, and the sheriff wants you children to come to the office. Nancy's calling the Renners and Browns too."

"Can we, Mom?" Josh asked. "We'll come right back home and work on our studies. We promise."

Mrs. Morgan laughed. "Far be it from me to deprive you of this ongoing learning experience. Just be careful."

"Let's go!" Josh said. "Maybe they caught the kidnapper!"

Josh and Emily raced for the garage to get their bicycles. Out in the street, they saw Carlos and Julie on their bikes, heading downtown too. The four children rode single file, talking loudly, wondering what might have happened. The streets were wet and filled with puddles since it had rained early that morning. The gray sky threatened more rain.

Billy and Becky were already at the sheriff's office when the other four arrived. The six children filed through the front door.

Nancy, the receptionist, smiled broadly at the children. Nancy was a member of their church. A year before, her car had died on the interstate highway outside of Springdale. Becky and Billy's mother had picked her up on the shoulder of the road and brought her home. They soon found out Nancy had no job. Her husband had abandoned her and her three children.

She and her children stayed with the Renners two months before she found a job at the sheriff's office as a secretary/receptionist. They lived with the Renners another two months before she found an apartment she could afford. Living with the Renners, she experienced God's love. After six months of attending church in Springdale, she became a Christian. Now she was eager to share the love of Jesus with those in need. She knew what it was like to feel hopeless and alone.

"Hello." Nancy was glad to see them. "I heard you all are regular detectives now. Sheriff Weaver said he might have to put you on the payroll."

"That's not what he called us about, is it?" Billy asked.

"I don't think so." Nancy had a twinkle in her eye. "But he does have some news."

"I'm glad you all got here so quickly," Sheriff Weaver said soberly as he walked into the room from his office.

"What happened?" Josh asked.

"Something happened last night that we're almost certain involved our kidnapper," the sheriff said solemnly.

"What? What?" Billy asked.

"Last night there was a fire out at the old Garner house. The place where you rescued Mr. Finley."

"Was anyone hurt?" Julie asked.

"Nope. No one was there. But we're sure the fire was set," the sheriff said.

"To destroy evidence?" Josh asked excitedly.

"Maybe, but we think there was another reason." The sheriff was grave. "When the fire started, we were short-handed, so we stopped the stakeout at the park. Our officer was gone several hours. While we were at the fire, someone was apparently looking for that treasure. Early this morning we found several more large holes dug around that big oak tree where Billy found the cup."

"Wow!" Billy said. "You think he set the fire to distract you?"

"Looks that way," Sheriff Weaver said matter-of-factly. "We would have been out there till dawn if that big rain hadn't come and helped us put the fire out. We had two inches of rain."

"Do you think whoever was digging found anything?" Josh asked.

"We don't think so," the sheriff said. "The holes aren't that deep, but there are several of them. Unfortunately, the rain washed away any footprints or tracks."

"Let's go out there and dig up the treasure before the thief finds it," Billy said.

"Personally I don't believe that the treasure is there," Sheriff Weaver said.

"Why not?" Josh asked.

"Because I talked to Sheriff Barns, who was sheriff

back then. He said that someone would have noticed a freshly dug hole big enough to bury a safe and other valuables along that path. The land wasn't a city park yet, but people traveled that path every day."

"But that's where the cup was found, the second cup, I mean," Josh said. "And the other cup was in that same area, right?"

"That's what the thief said," Sheriff Weaver replied.

"But he was the man who claimed he was innocent," Julie said.

"He was convicted along with his partner," Sheriff Weaver replied.

"But what if he was innocent and telling the truth all along?" Josh asked. "If he wasn't the third partner, then the real third partner might still be around looking for the treasure. He would know that the innocent man was telling the truth about the cup."

"I'm going to have to give these children badges and make them deputies," the sheriff said to Nancy. Sheriff Weaver smiled at the children.

"What they say could be right," Nancy replied.

"The shape of the evidence so far says it's possible," Josh said. "Don't you agree, Sheriff Weaver?"

"It's possible, but it's still inconclusive." He tugged on his gun belt.

"Are you still posting a stakeout to watch the tree?" Josh asked.

"We'll definitely patrol the area at night, but not as much during the day," the sheriff said. "I'm afraid we lost our best chance to catch whoever it was last night.

I'm sure he'll be more careful now. We'll talk to people that live along the lake and ask them to keep their eyes open for suspicious activity."

"What about the hobo we saw at the park the day Billy found the cup?" Josh asked.

"We're keeping an eye on him," the sheriff said.

"I'd just bet he's the one who's behind all this," Billy said harshly.

"He's an unusual fellow all right." The sheriff sounded uneasy. "We definitely have an interest in his relationship to this case since you kids noticed him hanging around."

"Are you going to arrest him?" Billy asked.

"We aren't ready to make an arrest yet," the sheriff said. Once again he seemed troubled. "We don't have enough evidence. But if we make an arrest, I'll be sure and let you kids know. I just have one more thing to tell you."

"What's that?" Julie asked.

"Be very careful, kids," Sheriff Weaver said seriously. "Whoever is interested in this treasure is dangerous, and maybe desperate. I don't want anyone to get hurt. Now you best run along and leave the case to us."

Chapter Eight

A
Fake
Beard

I don't get it." Billy was angry. "It's almost like
Sheriff Weaver doesn't want us on the case."

The home school detectives assembled on the
sidewalk in front of the sheriff's building and got their
bicycles. Billy knocked his kickstand up angrily. "It's
just not fair!" Billy seethed. He slapped the top of his
bike helmet.

"He didn't actually tell us to stop looking for clues,"
Josh said. "He just wants us to be careful, that's all."

"But he said that the crook was dangerous and desperate," Emily replied. "It seemed like he was telling us
to mind our own business."

"Well, I think we should keep our eyes and ears
open," Josh said. "After all, we've been involved with
this case from the start. We've got to go home and do
our studies. But let's meet at the park at 2:30 and look

at those holes by the oak tree. Maybe we can figure something out by then. Don't be late."

The others agreed that was the best plan. Josh and Emily rode home quickly. Mrs. Morgan had their lessons ready. The younger children, Elizabeth, David and Daniel, had already begun their studies.

Two rooms in the house were dedicated to schooling. Josh and Emily and Mr. and Mrs. Morgan had their library of books and supplies and computers in one room, while the younger children studied in another room. Mrs. Morgan spent more time with the younger children since they needed more direct attention and tutoring, especially with phonics and reading and math. While she was working with the younger ones, Josh and Emily started on their lessons. They began with Spanish and Latin, followed by writing and literature, math, history and geography, and science.

When the younger children's work was through, Mrs. Morgan monitored Josh and Emily's work and answered questions. She spent more time with them when they started a new unit or had trouble with a new concept. Since each child got direct tutoring, studying at home made for efficient use of time.

After lunch, they did their work on music and art and physical education while Mrs. Morgan evaluated their paperwork. Once their chores around the house were done, the children were free to concentrate on the activities they personally liked. Emily usually worked and played on the computer if she wasn't playing with her other friends who home schooled. Josh liked doing a variety of things on his own and with others. A few days earlier, he had been helping Carlos with some science experiments at Carlos's house. Some afternoons, the children in the home school co-op worked on projects together, like the leaf-collecting trip a few days before.

During lunch, it began raining. Josh was afraid they might have to cancel their trip to the park. It kept raining while they were practicing their music; but by the time they finished their chores around the house at 1:30, the rain finally stopped.

"You two are acting like caged animals." Mrs. Morgan knew they were anxious to leave. "Just make sure you're home by the time it gets dark. That means 5:30."

"Right, Mom," Emily said.

"I'll take the radios," Josh said to Emily. He put them in his backpack. "I have an idea."

Josh and Emily pedaled as hard as they could all the way to the park. The other kids were already waiting by the big oak tree. Everything was still wet from the rain. Molly, the Renners' dog, ran rapidly around the park, sniffing every tree, weed and rock.

"Wow!" Billy said when they got to the old oak tree below the bluff. Over a dozen holes, two feet deep or more, were scattered around the big tree. "Whoever was digging did some real work."

"He was careful too." Josh pointed to a pile of wet weeds. "It looks like he cut down all the poison ivy and raked it away before he started digging."

"You're right," Emily said. "He cleared off the ground."

"But there are no footprints," Carlos observed. "The rain washed everything away, like the sheriff said."

"I wonder where that strange guy is," Josh said. "I thought they would pick him up for questioning or something like that."

"I thought the sheriff acted kind of funny when you mentioned him," Julie said. "It sort of seemed like he didn't want to talk about him."

"I was thinking this morning that we should talk to him ourselves," Josh said boldly.

"What are you going to do? Ask him if he kidnapped Mr. Finley and was out here digging holes last night?" Emily asked with a grin. "Maybe you should just ask him to arrest himself too."

"Don't be funny," Josh said. "All we would do is just ask him if he's noticed anyone suspicious in the park. We could show him the story in the newspaper. I'm sure he won't admit he's guilty of anything, but maybe he would say something that would implicate him. Then we could tell Sheriff Weaver and he could maybe arrest him."

"Sounds far-fetched to me," Emily said.

"Do you have any better ideas?" Josh demanded.

"I've been thinking, and I have an idea too," Billy announced. "I think we should get my Uncle Jack's metal detector and walk around this tree with it."

"Metal detector?" Josh asked.

"Sure," Billy said. "My uncle uses it when he goes to the beach to look for coins and things. He found over twenty dollars one day. One time he found a lady's car keys. Another time he found a wedding ring. It's real sensitive. If there's a great big safe buried around here, that detector would find it for sure."

"That's a good idea, Billy," Josh said with admiration.

"Well, I think we should talk to people who live along the lake by the clubhouse and ask if they've seen anything suspicious," Emily said. "That's what real detectives do. They ask lots of questions. Maybe they noticed something last night or early this morning and didn't remember to tell the police."

"Now we are thinking like detectives!" Josh said eagerly. "Let's do it this way. We need to split up to make better use of our time. Carlos and I will go to the railroad bridge and see if we can talk to that guy with the gray beard."

"I can go get my uncle's metal detector," Billy said.

"Julie, Becky and I can talk to people in the lake houses," Emily said. "I'll keep my radio on, and you can let us know if you find that guy."

"Or in case we get into any trouble." Carlos was solemn.

"We'll be okay." But for an instant Josh felt a twinge of fear. "Let's meet back here in an hour or so."

They all took off on their bicycles. Josh and Carlos rode through old downtown Springdale. They had been riding ten minutes when Josh tried out the radio.

"WA5XCN, come in please?" Josh said into the radio. "WA5XCN, do you copy?"

"This is WA5XCN. I hear you, Josh," Emily said.

"Where are you?" Josh asked.

"We're down at the end of the lake," Emily said. "We're getting ready to go to the Thorndykes' house."

"Keep your radio turned on like we agreed," Josh said into the mouthpiece.

"Okay, WA5XNZ. I'll be standing by," Emily replied.

Josh and Carlos pedaled along Market Street, over to Bannister and then reached the road that ran along the railroad track.

They rode in silence. They passed woods and a scrubby brush area even though they were still in the Springdale city limits. They passed the old train depot, which was now used as a storage area for Jacob's Furniture Store. They passed what was left of the old grain silos.

Where the road curved and headed north, the railroad continued on straight over a long, dry riverbed. A small creek ran in the middle of the riverbed. Below the trestles was an odd assortment of little makeshift houses and old trailers. Several old, broken-down cars were parked in the area, as well as an old school bus, where Mrs. Carson lived. A few tents were set up in the distance.

A small campfire was burning by the first shack. A man was sitting near the fire, sewing a piece of leather into an old boot. The children had been there before with church members and knew that the man's first name was Johnny, but they didn't know his last name. He was an old man and was missing half his teeth. He always wore a faded denim jacket and blue jeans. His face was covered with gray stubble.

He smiled when he saw the children and looked a little surprised. "I thought the big party wasn't until this weekend." Johnny stood up slowly.

"It is," Carlos said. "You're coming, aren't you?"

"I sure am," Johnny said. "You folks have been awful nice to us out here."

"That's what God's love is like," Josh said simply. "What are you doing?"

"I'm working on this boot," Johnny said. "Trying to get a few more miles on it. These are Red Wings, you know. Real quality. They're worth fixing up."

Josh nodded, not sure what else to say. Another man came out of the closest shack. He had a blue windbreaker on.

"Did you all bring any food?" he asked.

"Not this time," Josh said.

"Oh." He looked disappointed, turned and went back into the shack.

"Jack may or may not go to your church party," Johnny said. "I guess it depends on if he's hungry and ain't drunk."

"He was invited, wasn't he?" Carlos asked.

"We were all invited," Johnny said. "Hey, I saw in the newspapers that you kids helped bust up a kidnapping. They said you acted like regular detectives. Did they catch the fellow that did it yet?"

"Not yet," Carlos said. "That's why we're out here."

"You think someone out here done it?" Johnny asked

eagerly. He sipped from a blue coffee mug. "I haven't heard anything. But it could be somebody out here I reckon. Most folks around here mind their own business."

"We aren't accusing anyone." Josh wanted to be careful. "But we have seen one man that was acting suspicious a few times. We thought you might know something about him."

"What's he look like?" Johnny asked.

"He's got a gray beard and a gray mustache," Josh said. "He's usually wearing a red plaid shirt."

"Tall, thin fellow?" Johnny asked.

"Yes," Billy said. "Do you know him?"

"Know of him," Johnny said. "He showed up around here a week ago. Had his own tent. A pretty fancy tent and cook stove. Stayed here three nights maybe and then left. Haven't seen him since."

"You mean he's not here anymore?" Carlos was plainly disappointed.

"Just disappeared," the old man said.

"Where's he from? Do you know his name?" Josh asked.

"Said his name was Bob." Johnny rubbed his grizzled cheek. "He was an odd one. Tightlipped, hardly said a word. He stayed in his tent most evenings. Left during the day. Mrs. Carson watched his stuff while he was gone so no one would steal it."

"Does she know him?"

"Better than me," Johnny said. "Maybe she can tell you about him. Him and his fake beard."

"Fake beard?" Billy asked.

"That's right," Johnny said. "Mrs. Carson's got three little kids, you know, and they're regular snoops. Well, they were snooping around Bob's fancy tent and one of them went inside when his mother wasn't looking, and he said he found a little suitcase full of lipsticks and mirrors and all kinds of doo-dads to dress yourself up like Halloween."

"Sounds like a makeup case," Josh said.

"That's what Mrs. Carson said it was. She found her kids playing with it. She made them put it back just like they found it. But she said there was gray hair inside the case. A wig of hair. And even a beard wig or whatever you'd call it."

"A fake beard?" Josh asked.

"That's what she told me. But you should go ask her," the old man said.

Josh and Carlos went down to the old bus. They knocked on the folding doors, but no one answered. The boys walked back up to the campfire where Johnny sat working on his boot. He poured himself another cup of coffee, then set the pot back down near the fire.

"She didn't answer when we knocked on the bus doors," Josh said.

"Maybe she went to town with Eddy Fry. A bunch of them left this morning in his car," the old man said. "I knew there was something fishy about that new guy. I couldn't put my finger on it before. But he shook my hand when we first met."

"What's so odd about that?"

"Well, it was his hand."

Johnny looked down at his own worn palm. "His hand was soft and nice. Men that live around here don't have hands like that. I looked down and noticed that his fingernails were cut perfect and clean. No dirt in them. But his face and clothes were dirty. That man Bob isn't what he appears to be. He's a strange one all right. You kids be careful if you're messing around with him."

Josh nodded. He and Carlos were just getting onto their bikes when Emily's voice came over the radio.

"WA5XNZ, come in, come in, Josh," Emily said. Her voice was strained and excited.

"This is WA5XNZ," Josh said. "What's wrong, Emily?"

"You need to get back to the park quick, Josh," Emily said.

"What's wrong?" Josh demanded.

"Just hurry, Josh," Emily said. "I have to go now. Hurry before it's too late!"

"Emily! Emily!" Josh yelled into the radio. All he heard was the empty crackle and static.

Chapter Nine

Break-In

Josh and Carlos pedaled as fast as they could back to the park. Both boys were breathing hard as they sped into Springdale Park. Beyond the clubhouse, they saw Emily and the other girls. Since they appeared to be okay, Josh gave a sigh of relief. He rode over to the girls.

"What's going on?" Josh demanded as he skidded to a halt.

"It was the gray-haired man," Emily said. "We think we saw him breaking into a house on the lake."

"Breaking in?" Josh asked.

"Yes," Emily said. "We started at the house at the end of the lake and worked our way toward the clubhouse. But when we got to that yellow house down there, I saw him. He was walking along the lake, kind of slinking along real suspiciously. He even stood behind some bushes before he went to the back door. I ran around the side of the Baileys' house to watch him. He fiddled with the back door lock, but he finally got the door to open. Then he went inside."

"That's it?" Josh asked.

"Isn't that enough?" Emily asked. "We've been standing here watching the house ever since. Billy is down by the lake watching the back entrance so he can't get away."

"He didn't break any windows or anything?" Josh asked.

"No," Emily said.

"He didn't even see us watching him," Julie said. "At least I don't think he did."

"You know that bum doesn't live in that house," Becky said. "I just bet he's up to no good."

"Whose house is it?" Josh asked.

"We think you and Emily should go ask the people playing bingo who lives there," Becky said. "When you find out, call Sheriff Weaver and tell him about it."

"I guess we could try that," Josh said. "The more we learn about that man, the more suspicious he seems."

"What if he's the third thief and he's come back for the treasure?" Becky asked.

"Let's go ask a few questions," Josh said.

Josh and Emily went inside the Lake Club House while Carlos, Julie and Becky watched the yellow house. Billy stayed down by the lake watching the rear of the home.

The clubhouse was filled with people playing bingo

and working on crafts. Mrs. Witherspoon and Mrs. Petticoat were in the corner near the front door working at a quilting frame.

"There are our star detectives now!" Mrs. Witherspoon had a beaming smile on her face. She waved the children over.

"You children did a brave thing helping Mr. Finley like that," Mrs. Petticoat said with admiration.

"A very brave thing," Mrs. Witherspoon added.

"It wasn't that much," Josh said modestly. He cleared his throat. "Say, do either of you happen to know who lives in that yellow house just down by the lake?"

"The yellow house?" Mrs. Petticoat asked. "Why, that belongs to Sheriff Barns. He uses it more as a summer house than as his regular home."

"Sheriff Barns?" Josh asked in surprise.

"That's right," Mrs. Witherspoon said. "He's retired now, but he was the sheriff for years. He was sheriff back when the Springdale Shelter robbery took place."

"Yes, we know," Emily said. "And you're sure that's his house?"

"Well, you can ask him if you want," Mrs. Petticoat said. "He's right over there playing bingo."

Josh looked across the room. Sheriff Barns was sitting right next to Mr. Thorndyke. He was laughing with the others at his table. Josh walked over.

"Sheriff Barns?" Josh asked. The retired sheriff looked up. He squinted at Josh as if trying to remember something.

"It's the boy detective!" Sheriff Barns announced to

the others. Everyone smiled and congratulated Josh.

"Could I speak to you?" Josh asked. "Privately."

"Well, sure." The retired sheriff got up from the table and walked over to Josh. "What's on your mind, son?"

"We think a strange man broke into your house on the lake a little while ago," Josh whispered.

"Strange man?" the sheriff asked. "What did he look like?"

"He's got gray hair and a gray mustache," Josh said. "He kind of looks like a bum or one of those homeless men down at the railroad bridge."

"Oh, him." The sheriff looked uneasy for a moment but then smiled. "He's not breaking in. He's a man who's helping me around the place."

"He's helping you?" Josh asked in surprise.

"Look, son, don't worry about that man." The sheriff was serious. "And I'd appreciate it if you wouldn't tell the other folks around here about him either. He's sort of part of a surprise I've got planned."

"A surprise?" Josh asked. "What kind of surprise?"

"Well, it wouldn't be a surprise if I told, now would it?" the old sheriff said with a big smile. Then his face got very serious, and he leaned in closer to Josh and whispered, "Just leave well enough alone. Okay, son? And you kids forget what you saw."

The sheriff smiled once more and went back to the table with his friends. Josh backed away, feeling more confused than ever. He crossed the room to Emily, who was listening to Mrs. Witherspoon.

"It was horrible, horrible what those thieves did,"

Mrs. Witherspoon said. "I tell you, when I heard that Mr. Smoot died in prison, I wasn't the least bit sorry for him. My mother donated her best china to that auction. It sold to some prominent citizens over in Milam County, as I remember."

"That awful crime gave Springdale a black eye as a community," Mrs. Petticoat added. "Sometimes problems bring out the best in people, but in this case it brought out the worst. Once that robbery happened, people began to bicker about all sorts of things, blaming and accusing. Good people who should have known better were acting like enemies instead of neighbors. A dark cloud settled over this whole town."

"I don't know if I'd agree to that," Mrs. Witherspoon sniffed.

"Well, no one ever took up a collection as successful as that one ever again," Mrs. Petticoat said. "And I thought it was shameful what happened to all those poor folks out at Shantytown."

"What happened?" Emily asked. "We read about that place in the newspapers, but they just mentioned the name. I couldn't find any other stories about it."

"I'm not surprised," Mrs. Petticoat said. "No one in town wants to own up to what happened."

"What did happen?" Josh asked.

"Shantytown was actually not too far from here," Mrs. Petticoat said. "It was near the south end of the lake. A lot of real poor people stayed there. In fact, part of the city park land we have now used to be what they called Shantytown. It really wasn't a town but some old leftover military barracks from World War II and several tiny little shacks. After the robbery, a lot of people were angry because the thieves had lived out at Shantytown. A bunch of people got together and went out and tore the whole place down. One of the men in the group was on the city council, and he claimed he had the legal right to do it."

"He did have a legal right," Mrs. Witherspoon rebutted.

"Even so, it could have been handled differently," Mrs. Petticoat replied. "I think they acted like a mob. It all happened so fast. The bulldozers showed up one morning, and the whole place was gone by noon."

"Well, it was city property, and they had a right," Mrs. Witherspoon retorted. "After all, the place was a mess. It was infested with rats bigger than alley cats, I heard. My uncle was out there the day they tore it down. He said they were planning on tearing it down for a long time anyway."

"But where did all those poor people go?" Mrs. Petticoat responded. "I heard those folks were scurrying out of the back door carrying anything they could grab while the bulldozers were smashing down the front door. I just don't think it was handled right. Those people were left on the street. And it wasn't just old bums, but families."

"Where did they go?" Josh asked.

"I don't know." Mrs. Petticoat sounded sad. "They just moved on, I guess."

"Well, you can't have people living like animals," Mrs. Witherspoon said. "One of the reasons they tore the place down was that they were hoping to find that missing safe."

"Did they find anything?" Josh asked.

"Not a thing," Mrs. Petticoat said. "I think looking for that safe was just an excuse."

"Everyone wanted to find that treasure back then," Mrs. Witherspoon said.

"Someone is still wanting to find the treasure," Emily said. "Someone dug several holes by that tree below the bluff in the middle of the night. We think it may be the thief."

"Nothing would surprise me when there's lots of money involved," Mrs. Witherspoon said.

"We're going to use a metal detector and look around down below the bluff," Josh said.

"You remember to be careful playing around that bluff," Mrs Witherspoon said. "A boy in my third-grade class fell off it one time and broke his leg in three places. He had a limp for the rest of his life. Avery Garner was his name."

"That bluff is dangerous," Mrs. Petticoat agreed. "We used to play there a long time ago when we were just kids. There was no park here then, of course, though the cemetery was still in the same place."

"I was always scared of that cemetery when I was a little girl," Mrs. Witherspoon replied. "But you had to walk through it to get to the lake way back then."

"My brothers and I used to play in the cave on the bluff," Mrs. Petticoat said fondly. "Then we'd go swimming."

"I didn't know there was a cave on the bluff," Josh said.

"You aren't supposed to know," Mrs. Petticoat said. "Parents were afraid kids would get hurt, so they filled it in. It wasn't a big cave really. That was a long time ago, back during the Depression, before World War II."

"My parents didn't even want me to play around the bluff or at the lake," Mrs. Witherspoon said. "They thought I'd get bitten by a snake."

"Well, we better go." Josh motioned to Emily. He was afraid the two older ladies would talk their ears off. "Our friends are waiting outside. We've been asking people along the lake if they've seen any suspicious activity since Billy found the cup."

"You should talk to Mr. Craven," Mrs. Petticoat said. "He lives right next door. I bet he's interested in this case. After all, he worked in city hall back then. He was the manager of the records department."

"I read about him in the newspaper," Josh said. "At the trial he testified that Arnold Baker was drunk on the job and that he had him fired."

"He usually comes to these meetings," Mrs. Witherspoon said. "I wonder why he's not here today."

"He had some allergy problem," Mrs. Petticoat replied. "That's what he told Mr. Crumley."

"That's odd. I didn't know he suffered from allergies," she said. "Usually wild horses couldn't keep him away from playing bingo. You might see if he has anything to add."

"We'll talk to him." Josh, anxious to get out the door,

was beginning to think he would never get away from the two ladies.

"You children deserve a medal, I think," Mrs. Petticoat said.

Josh smiled. When he looked up, he saw the retired Sheriff Barns staring across the room straight back at him. The old man wasn't smiling.

Chapter Ten

What Molly Found

O nce outside, Josh called everyone to the clubhouse parking lot, including Billy and their
dog Molly.

"Shouldn't I be watching the back of the
house in case that weird guy tries to get away?" Billy
asked.

"I don't know what to think," Josh replied honestly.
"The more I hear, the less I understand about this whole
case."

He quickly told the others what he and Carlos learned
talking to Johnny out at the old railroad bridge. Then he
told them what Sheriff Barns said.

"Sheriff Barns knows the guy?" Billy asked in surprise. "Something weird is going on here."

"That's for sure," Josh said.

"Do you think Sheriff Barns knows something he's

not telling?" Carlos asked.

"I'm sure of it," Josh replied. "But what?"

"I wonder if he and that homeless guy are working together," Julie asked. Everyone was quiet. They all thought the same thing at the same time.

"Do you think old Sheriff Barns is doing something illegal?" Billy asked.

"He's acting awful strange, that's for sure," Josh said. "I don't know what to think. He was sheriff back then. I suppose he could have been involved in the robbery in some way."

"But then who's that strange guy, and why is he staying at his house?" Billy asked.

"Maybe he's some kind of blackmailer or something," Carlos said. "I saw a story like that on television once, about a crooked cop and a blackmailer. Only this cop was involved in selling drugs."

"Wow!!" Billy said.

"Hold on," Josh said. "We can't jump to conclusions here. I think we need to do what we planned. Let's use Billy's metal detector around the tree before it gets dark and see if we find anything."

"Mrs. Witherspoon said we should talk to Mr. Craven," Emily said. "We've stopped at all the houses along the lake except his and Sheriff Barns's."

"Okay, but let's make it quick," Josh said.

The children ran over to Mr. Craven's house. They knocked on the door. After a minute, it opened a crack. The old man had a beaked nose and thinning white hair. He glared through the crack at the children.

"What do you want?" he demanded.

"Mr. Craven, I'm Josh Morgan and these are my—"

"I know who you are." Mr. Craven sounded impatient. "I read the newspaper."

"Well, we were wondering if we could talk to you about the robbery that happened thirty years ago," Josh said.

"Talk to me? What for?"

"Well, since you worked at city hall and knew some of the thieves, we thought you might be able to give us some more information. We also wanted to ask you if you've noticed any—"

"Shouldn't you kids be in school?"

"We're home schooled," Julie said.

"That's right. I forgot," the man said. Billy looked intently at the red patches on the old man's hands.

"I've been rather sick lately." The man pulled down his shirtsleeves.

"They said at the clubhouse that you were having some problems with allergies," Emily said sympathetically.

"That's right, I am," the old man said. "And I don't have time to answer a lot of questions about something that happened thirty years ago. Just because some fool robs an antique owner doesn't mean there's any missing treasure. That money was spent a long time ago."

"But why do you think someone tried to dig up all around the big oak tree by the bluff?" Josh asked. "Someone must think the treasure is still around. We wondered if you saw anyone digging over there or hanging around the bluff since you have such a good view. Of course, I guess the police already asked you that."

"The police haven't asked me anything," the old man said.

"They haven't?" Emily asked. "All the houses we stopped at said the deputy had been by asking if anyone noticed any suspicious activity around the bluff."

"Well, they haven't been here," the old man grumbled.

"Well, if you do see anything, I'm sure they'd want you to call," Julie said.

"That treasure's been gone for thirty years," Mr. Craven said. "You kids got everyone riled up over nothing."

"We think the treasure may still be there," Billy said. "We're going over by the oak tree to look for it with a metal detector."

"Metal detector?" The old man stared at the long, polelike object in Billy's hand curiously.

"Yeah, if there's treasure there, this should find it," Billy said eagerly.

"All that you kids will find is poison ivy," the old man said. "I'd stay away from there if I were you, and quit pestering folks with a lot of foolish questions about stuff that's been over and done with for thirty years. Kids like you should be in school like everybody else. Good day to you."

With that, Mr. Craven shut the door firmly in their faces. Josh turned around and shrugged his shoulders at the other children.

"He wasn't very friendly," Becky said.

"Maybe he acts that way because he's sick," Julie said. "My great aunt Martha gets real cranky when her arthritis acts up, but most of the time she's real pleasant."

"He acts like we shouldn't even be interested in solving the case," Billy said.

"Let's get over to the tree and try the detector out before it gets dark," Josh said.

"I know I'm ready," Billy said. The home school detectives hopped on their bikes and rode swiftly over to the big oak tree by the bluff. Everything was soaked from the rain. Josh looked at the holes in the ground for a long time.

Not too far away, a pair of binoculars was trained on the children standing around the old oak tree. The children were too busy getting ready to search the ground to notice the watching eyes.

Molly ran through the woods and brush, sniffing the ground. She began barking as she ran around the bottom of the bluff. A rabbit suddenly shot out of the weeds around the big oak tree, scampered across the trail and disappeared into the shrubs and weeds at the base of the bluff. Molly yelped and took off after the rabbit.

"Molly, come back!" Becky yelled. But the big dog was too busy to notice.

"She'll come back," Billy said.

"But she'll hurt the poor little bunny," Becky said.

"She couldn't catch that rabbit if she tried," Billy said.

"She sure is trying hard." Josh smiled. "How did she

get way up there?" Josh pointed. Way up the side of the bluff they could see Molly's tail wagging among the brush on the ledges of rock.

"She must be part mountain goat," Carlos said. The dog's barking got fainter, and then faded altogether. The kids turned back to the tree.

"Watch out for that poison ivy," Josh warned. "Let's use the metal detector."

The children took turns using the metal detector. After thirty minutes, it only sounded once. When they dug at that spot, all they found was a flattened, rusty can.

"I don't think anything is here," Josh said.

"Me neither," the others said with discouragement.

"What have you got, Molly?" Billy asked. Molly walked up slowly carrying an old red piece of cloth. Becky took it out of the dog's mouth and patted her head.

"You didn't catch a bunny but some old shirt," Becky said. "Where did you get this? I hope you aren't stealing stuff." Molly wagged her tail with pride.

"Let me see it," Josh said. Becky handed him the shirt. He looked at the collar for a label. But as he pulled it open, the shirt came apart in his hands. Dusty red particles fell on his hands.

"This thing is totally rotten." Josh was disgusted. He dropped it on the ground. He slapped his hands together, making puffs of red, smoky lint.

"Don't litter." Emily picked it up and put it on the seat of one of the bicycles.

Just then, the alarm sounded on the metal detector. Billy and Carlos immediately began digging. Everyone crowded around. They all groaned when Billy uncovered another old soft drink can. He threw the can back into the hole. As he stooped to pick up the shovel, he slipped and fell in the mud.

"Billy!" his sister yelped. "Look at that mess."

"Yuck, this mud is horrible." Billy tried to wipe it off with his hands.

"You're really going to be in trouble," Becky said. "Just look at you."

"Use this rag. It's dry," Carlos said.

"Lucky for you that Molly brought you a dry rag to clean yourself off with," Emily said. "She's a real servant. We should put her in our servants' class at church."

"Yeah," Julie added. "But how did Molly find a dry rag when everything around here is soaked? She's must be part bloodhound."

"Wait!" Josh cried out. "Let me see that rag."

"But I'm all muddy," Billy protested.

"I'll give it to you in a minute," Josh said. "After we check this out."

"Check what out?" Emily asked.

"This shirt. Don't you see?" Josh pointed at the bluff. "Molly brought this shirt from up there on the bluff. Everything is soaking wet around here."

"So what?" Emily asked.

"But this shirt is dry," Josh replied. "What does that tell you?"

"It tells me I'm lucky because Molly brought me a dry shirt to wipe off all this mud," Billy replied. "Now let me have it."

Billy reached out for the shirt, but Josh pulled it back. Josh smiled.

"I see what you're saying," Emily said. "How did Molly find this dry shirt when everything else is wet?"

All the children looked at each other and then looked up at the bluff. Molly wagged her tail, watching the children.

"Remember what Mrs. Witherspoon said?" Josh asked.

"Said about what?" Billy asked. "I don't get it. She said lots of things."

"She said that when they were kids, they used to play in a cave on the bluff," Josh replied.

"That's right!" Emily added. "But she said they filled it in."

"She said they covered it up or filled it in," Josh said firmly. "She wasn't sure. But maybe that's where Molly found the shirt. It makes sense."

"She probably just dug it out of some rabbit hole," Billy said.

"I'm going to check it out." Josh started up the side of the hill.

"Me too," Emily replied.

"But it's almost dark," Julie yelled after them.

"That's why we need to look now," Josh said. "Let's go. Here, Molly. Here, girl!" The dog ran eagerly up the bluff after Josh.

"I still don't get it," Billy said. "What's the big deal about an old, rotten shirt?"

He began climbing up the hill after the others. Josh

was halfway up the steep bluff when he saw the small tracks of a rabbit in the mud along with the larger tracks of a dog.

"Here, Molly. Here, girl," Josh called. Molly ran to the older boy. He patted the ground. The big dog sniffed the ground and wagged her tail.

"Go fetch. Fetch, girl." Julie was excited.

The dog didn't seem to know what to do at first. But then she sniffed the rabbit track and sniffed the next one and began climbing up between the rocks.

"Let her go on her own." Josh watched the dog. Little by little, Molly wound her way up the side of the bluff. She jumped up on a ledge of rock and disappeared behind a boulder and cedar tree.

"Let's go," Josh said. Single file, the children climbed carefully up the side of the bluff. When they got to the big boulder and cedar tree, Josh slipped on loose rocks and mud. He fell back onto Emily and Julie, who struggled to steady him.

"Whoa!" Josh tried to regain his balance. "That was too close. If you fell from here, you wouldn't stop rolling until you reached the lake."

The children looked down behind them. They were surprised to see how high they'd come.

"Be careful," Julie said. "Someone could really get hurt."

Josh pulled himself up on the big boulder and then helped the others up. When they were standing on the big, flat ledge, they heard barking still above them.

"Molly is on the next ledge," Billy said. "But how

did she get up there?" The ledge of limestone jutted out over the children's heads.

"There must be a hole or path or something," Josh said. "Molly can't fly."

"Over there." Carlos pointed beyond a big cedar tree.

Josh and the others carefully walked to the edge of the big boulder. There was a crack in the limestone ledge above them. Halfway up the ledge, mud had collected in a hollow spot in the rock with Molly's telltale footprint in the middle. Josh started climbing up through the crack. As he poked his head up above the next ledge, he saw Molly, or at least the rear half of her. Her head was down in a hole. The sound of her barking was muffled.

"She's up here." Once again Josh helped the rest of the children up until they were all standing on a rock ledge.

"Molly, what did you find?" Billy asked. The big golden retriever pulled her head out of a large hole.

"I think your dog may have just found a secret cave." Josh was grinning with excitement.

Chapter Eleven

In
the
Cave

Everyone crowded around the hole. Molly wagged her tail happily.

"It's just a hole, I bet." Becky sounded disappointed.

"I think it's the old cave." Josh got down on his hands and knees and stuck his head in the hole.

"What do you see? What do you see?" Billy demanded.

Josh pulled his head out. He turned to the others and smiled.

"It's a hole big enough for someone to sit in."

"But that can't be a cave," Carlos said. "It's too little."

"Mrs. Witherspoon said they covered it up," Josh said. "Help me clear out some of this brush."

Josh began quickly pulling back the brush and small rocks. As the hole grew larger, they uncovered a hard, sharp edge.

"That's an unusually straight rock," Carlos observed.

"That's no rock. That's sheet iron," Josh replied excitedly. He pulled on the edge of the metal, but it wouldn't budge. Carlos went over to help Josh pull, but neither of them could move it.

"We'll never move that," Billy said. "All those big rocks are on top of that piece of metal."

"Then there must be another way," Josh said. A large rock blocked the other side of the hole. Josh began digging around the rock.

"That's part of the cliff," Julie said.

"No, it's not," Josh said. "Look at that edge. This is a large, flat rock."

"Let's get the shovels," Billy said. In a moment, Billy and Josh and Julie were headed back down the bluff. In five minutes, they struggled back up the bluff and began to dig. Little by little they uncovered the edges of a large, flat rock.

"Let's try it now." Josh stuck the shovel in the hole and braced it. Using the handle as a lever, he began pushing. "Help me."

Billy and Julie pushed on the handle. The rock began to move, just a half an inch at first. Then suddenly it was on its edge.

"Watch out!" Josh yelled as the rock flopped onto the limestone ledge.

"Wow!" Billy said. "Look at that hole!"

A gaping hole, over four feet high, led into the side of the cliff. The setting sun was in just the right angle to shine into the cave. On the dry rock inside Josh saw rabbit droppings and a rabbit nest. Further inside they saw a flash of light.

Sitting on a big boulder in the middle of the cave was an old wooden crate. Inside the crate they saw the top of a large golden teapot glittering in the light of the setting sun. Josh whooped for joy.

Billy reached the crate first. Even though it was dusty, the golden tea set was beautiful. Julie picked up a cup and turned it over. *George W. Baniston* was etched firmly on the bottom.

"This is it. This is it!" Julie shrieked. The children picked up the big teapot, a golden tray, a creamer, a sugar holder, and seven cups and eight saucers. All had the same name on the bottom. The rest of the crate was empty except for an old black Bible.

"See, one cup is missing," Billy said. "The one I found. But where's the rest of the treasure? Where's the safe and all the other stuff they took?"

"One cup?" Josh said. "There should be two cups missing, shouldn't there? The one they found thirty years ago and the one we found."

"That's right," Julie said. "That's odd. But maybe there's more stuff here."

The children searched eagerly around the cave, which was about the size of an ordinary bedroom. From floor to wall to ceiling, all they saw was solid rock. There were no other passageways or holes in the room. They found some old blankets, three empty whiskey bottles, a shovel and an empty canteen.

"Here's a Bible." Julie reached into the crate. She held up an old, black, hardback Bible and opened it. "It's a King James Version, the kind the Gideons donate."

"Let's see it." Josh held it and shook it.

"What are you doing?" Billy asked.

"Seeing if there are any letters or notes or any identification in it," Josh said. But when nothing fell out of the Bible, he shrugged his shoulders and put it back down in the crate.

"At least we found the set," Julie said.

"But there should be a lot more than this." Josh was frustrated. "I thought we would find the safe or more treasure."

"He didn't hide it in here, that's for sure," Billy said. "This place is solid rock."

"But it doesn't add up," Josh said. "This is part of the treasure. Remember the news accounts? They said they found the man without his shirt and all sweaty."

"And drunk," Emily added.

"I figured he was sweaty from stashing the stuff up here," Josh said.

"But how could they carry a safe up here?" Billy asked. "It was hard enough to climb up here without carrying anything. They never could have gotten a safe up here."

Julie picked up the Bible and opened the front cover. She looked in the back cover.

"Here's some writing," she said. On the inside page of the back cover were three rectangles drawn with a pencil. On the rectangle on the right were two Scripture references: "Genesis 3:19. Matthew 10:29-31." A large *X* in pencil was under the scriptures.

"Let me see." Josh looked at the references. "No name or map in here, is there?"

"I guess not," Julie said. "But I wonder why there are boxes like that?"

"Probably just somebody was making doodles," Billy said. "I like to make doodles."

"But not in your Bible," Becky said.

"Those scriptures look familiar somehow," Julie said slowly. "And I don't think they're just doodles. I've got a feeling they are important."

"Why don't we look them up?" Carlos asked. He knew that Julie's intuition about things was often right.

Josh opened the Bible to Genesis 3:19 and read: "In the sweat of thy face shalt thou eat bread, till thou return unto the ground; for out of it wast thou taken: for dust thou art, and unto dust shalt thou return."

"What's the Matthew scripture say?" Carlos asked.

Josh flipped the pages for a moment and stopped at Matthew 10:29-31. "Are not two sparrows sold for a farthing? And one of them shall not fall on the ground without your Father. But the very hairs of your head are all numbered. Fear not, therefore; ye are of more value than many sparrows."

Josh looked at the verses silently and then closed the Bible. He gave it to Julie. She looked at the three rectangles closely.

"Those seem like odd scriptures to put together," Billy said.

"The Genesis verse is like one that you would hear at a funeral," Becky remarked.

"Yeah," Josh agreed.

"I know I've seen those verses before." Julie tried to remember.

"Of course you have," Billy said. "They're in the Bible."

"No, I mean together like that." Julie took off her glasses and wiped the lenses slowly with her shirttail, thinking.

"We better go tell the sheriff what we found," Josh said. "I know he'll want to—"

"I've got it!" Julie blurted out. "On the graves. I saw it on those graves in the cemetery which said 'Unknown Man.' Remember the day Billy found the cup? Emily and I were looking at the graves of those unknown men. One of the gravestones had those two scriptures engraved on it."

"Oh, yeah," Emily said. "Didn't you make a sketch of those graves?"

"Yes," Julie said. "I forgot. I had been sketching different leaves, but I also made a sketch of the gravestones and the tree behind them." Julie found the sketchbook in her backpack. She turned through the pages quickly. "Here it is. 'Unknown Man.' There are the graves and Scripture references. And the dates on the tombstone."

"Look at that date," Josh said eagerly. "That's a week before the Springdale Shelter robbery."

"I bet it's those two men mentioned in the newspaper," Julie said. "Remember that the newspaper said that a train wreck killed two homeless men and no one ever claimed their bodies. They were buried that week."

"But why would that be in this Bible?" Carlos asked. No one said anything for a moment.

Then Josh's eyes lit up. "Maybe this is a kind of treasure map. The newspaper said Clifford Smoot dug graves sometimes for work, didn't it?"

"That's right," Emily said. "I understand what you're saying. The bodies might have been buried the same day as the robbery."

"And he might have buried the safe in the grave," Josh said. "No one would think it odd to see freshly dug dirt around those graves."

There was silence in the cave. Josh stared at the others. Each child began to smile.

"We need to go see Sheriff Weaver right away," Josh said.

"Wouldn't you rather go to the cemetery first?" a voice asked. The children whirled around. A figure blocked the entrance of the cave. A green ski mask covered his face. A black revolver was gripped in his hand. He pointed the barrel straight at Josh.

Chapter Twelve

Digging
a
Grave

You kids are better snoops than I figured," the man said tersely. "I was never sure if the treasure was still around or not . . . until that cup showed up."

"Lord Jesus, help us!" Julie whispered as she stared at the gun.

"Ha, ha! I've been praying too," the man grunted. "That cup showed up like an answer to a thirty-year-old prayer."

"You won't get away with this," Josh said evenly. "That treasure doesn't belong to you."

"So you intend to keep it?" the man asked and laughed.

"Of course not," Josh said. "It belongs to the town of Springdale, to the whole community."

"You're such a good citizen," the man said sarcasti-

gun. Billy stared at the man and watched him scratching.

"You can quit trying to disguise your voice, Mr. Craven," Billy said. "I know it's you."

"What?" the man hissed. He jerked back for an instant, as if startled.

"Billy, how do you—" Josh started to ask.

"Look at his hands," Billy said. "They're covered with poison ivy, just like Mr. Craven's hands when we saw him at his house."

"That's right," Becky said.

"You begin to notice other people's itches when you're itchy yourself," Billy said.

The man reached up and quickly pulled off the green ski mask. Mr. Jasper Craven smiled wickedly, still holding the gun.

"That thing was itchy, anyway," Mr. Craven said. "But of course, now that you know who I am, things are more complicated. But we'll cross that bridge later. Now we have work to do. The treasure is waiting."

Mr. Craven made the children walk down out of the cave single file. Billy led the way down the steep side of the bluff. He was forced to walk slowly since it had gotten dark.

"Don't try to be heroes or your friend here will be the first to go." Mr. Craven pushed the revolver into Josh's back.

Once down the bluff, they walked slowly through the park, without speaking, to Mr. Craven's house. He had the children load their shovels into his red Dodge Caravan. Then they all got inside. He drove slowly up to the cemetery, one hand on the steering wheel and the other holding the revolver that was aimed at Josh in the passenger seat.

He drove through the cemetery gate and down past the rows of gravestones until they reached the back of the cemetery. He parked in front of the gravestone that simply said "Unknown Man." The children got out of the car reluctantly. Mr. Craven kept the revolver aimed at Josh. He left the van running and the lights on.

"Use your metal detector in front of the grave with the two scriptures," Mr. Craven commanded. Billy frowned. He turned on the metal detector and swept it above the ground. As soon as he got close to the grave, the detector began blaring loudly.

"Bingo!" Mr. Craven smiled greedily. "You boys start digging."

"You won't get away with this." Josh picked up the shovel.

"Yes, I will," Mr. Craven said smugly. "Now quit stalling and dig!"

Josh wanted to argue but decided against it. He and Carlos began digging, while the others stood in a small group to one side. Josh prayed frantically as he shoveled, trying to figure out a way to get free.

"I should have known to look here," Mr. Craven said. "I went to visit Clifford Smoot in prison, but he wanted to keep double-crossing me, just like he double-crossed that poor Arnie Baker. He tricked us all."

At a depth of two feet, Josh's shovel hit something hard and metallic. Mr. Craven walked forward eagerly.

"Turn on your flashlight!" he ordered Emily. She did as she was told and shined the light down in the grave.

"Clear it off!" the old man demanded. Josh began digging around the metal. In a few minutes he had uncovered a two-and-a-half-foot-square plate. A smile spread across the face of the old man.

"The safe," he whispered. "Keep digging, keep digging."

"This doesn't belong to you." Anger was rising in Josh's voice.

"Finders keepers." The old man laughed. "And once we dig up the treasure, I'll have a nice big grave to put your bodies in. With a little luck, no one will find out about you kids for another thirty years. That's what happens to little snoops."

"Hold it right there!" a voice called out. The old man whirled around. Three men stood next to Mr. Craven's van. Sheriff Weaver was holding a pistol. Sheriff Barns held a shotgun. The third man was the bum who had been in Sheriff Barns's house. Mr. Craven looked at the three men in disbelief. He looked sadly back at the hole in the ground and then dropped his gun on the mound of freshly dug dirt.

Chapter Thirteen

The Party Begins

The next day, everyone met down at the sheriff's office. All three families were there, as well as Mr. Finley and Mrs. Highsmith from the newspaper. The retired Sheriff Barns sat in a chair near Sheriff Weaver, who was all smiles.

Josh and the other home school detectives crowded around the sheriff's desk. Standing behind the desk was another man who looked vaguely familiar, but Josh couldn't quite place him. The piercing blue eyes didn't fool Julie.

"You're that homeless man who was following us around," Julie said. "But what happened to your beard and mustache?"

The man reached down and picked up a small blue case. He opened it. Inside were several bottles and tubes and brushes.

"A makeup case," Julie said. "But why?"

"Kids, meet Robert Hastings, Jr.," said Sheriff Weaver. "We didn't have time to go into all this last night, but this is the man who called me about Jasper Craven and you kids. He's been keeping an eye on you kids and Jasper all along, ever since Billy found that cup."

"You children did a great job in helping me clear my father's name." Robert Hastings smiled.

"Your father?" Carlos asked.

"My father was one of the men accused of stealing the Springdale Shelter money," Mr. Hastings said. "After he got out of jail, he was never the same. Ten years away from your family is a long time, especially when my sister and I were so young."

"You used to live in Springdale?" Josh asked.

"Thirty years ago my family lived here," Mr. Hastings said. "But after the robbery, the bulldozers came and knocked everything down at Shantytown. My mother didn't think we should try to stay. We had no home, our father was in jail, and everyone in town thought she was married to a thief. It was a very hard time for us."

"How did this whole thing get started?" Josh asked. "I still don't understand about how Billy found the cup in the first place. I mean, in the cave, only one cup was missing from the tea service. But your father found the cup that was used at the trial. So where did the other cup come from?"

"You *are* a detective," Mr. Hastings smiled. He

reached down and lifted up a shiny golden cup. "This cup was the one at the trial and the same one Billy found by the oak tree. Sheriff Weaver found it in Jasper Craven's house this morning, hidden in a closet."

"I still don't understand," Josh said.

"After my father got out of jail, he wanted to forget everything about the robbery," Mr. Hastings said. "He never wanted to talk about it. He claimed that he was innocent but that no one would ever know. As I got older, I still couldn't forget what happened. I wanted to clear my father's name. I prayed and prayed about what to do. Last year, my father got sick and almost died from a stroke. After he recovered, he finally talked about being in jail. He said he overheard Clifford Smoot bragging about being rich once he got out. Of course, he never did get out because he died in jail. But while he was alive, Clifford had a visitor come see him twice. My father saw this visitor leaving the jail one day."

"Was that Arnie Baker?" Josh asked.

"No, we found the bones of Arnie Baker underneath the safe we dug up out of the grave," Sheriff Weaver said. "He had a knife stuck in his chest, murdered, we assume, by Clifford Smoot, thirty years ago."

"It must have been Mr. Craven that came to visit Clifford Smoot," Julie said.

"That's right," Mr. Hastings replied. "My father recognized him and concluded that he was the real third man involved in the robbery. After all, he worked at the city hall back then and had access to the keys. He was a respected citizen, and no one suspected him."

"But why didn't your father say something?" Josh asked.

"He knew he couldn't prove anything and assumed that no one would believe him," Mr. Hastings said simply. "And like I said, he wanted to forget the whole thing. But I didn't forget. I wanted to see justice done. That's when I thought of a plan."

"What plan?" Emily asked.

"I came to town and talked to Sheriff Barns about the case," Mr. Hastings said. "I told him what my father had said about Jasper Craven and the idea I had. Sheriff Barns let me have the original stolen cup, which had been stored all these years in a file cabinet. I left the cup by the old oak tree, praying that someone like you kids would find it and stir up interest in the case since it was the thirty-year anniversary of the robbery. If Jasper Craven thought the treasure was still around, I figured that he might tip his hand."

Mr. Hastings held up the cup and smiled. The shiny gold cup glistened. "Once Billy found the cup, things moved more quickly than I imagined," Mr. Hastings said. "I didn't anticipate that Jasper Craven would resort to kidnapping Mr. Finley. I was sure it was him, but there was still no hard evidence since he wasn't caught. I watched you kids using the metal detector around the tree and saw you go up the bluff to the cave. Then I saw Mr. Craven follow you. When I saw him holding the gun on Josh, I called Sheriff Weaver and Sheriff Barns immediately. We had to be careful since he had the gun. But he was so greedy to get the treasure that he got careless and didn't notice us coming from behind."

"But why did you wear the beard and mustache?" Julie asked.

"I look too much like my father did when he lived here thirty years ago," Mr. Hastings said. "I was afraid Jasper would recognize me and suspect something. Acting like a homeless person, I could hang out at the park near Jasper's house without his being suspicious."

"We were sure suspicious of you," Josh said. "I thought you were up to no good. I think you had us all fooled. But you got us out of a real jam."

"Well, I also helped you get into that jam," Robert Hastings said softly. "I'm really sorry that you kids and Mr. Finley were ever in danger. I just never realized that Jasper would get that desperate."

"God was taking care of us," Josh said confidently. "And I think God wanted to see justice done too. That's why your plan worked."

"Seeing my father's name cleared after all these years is a blessing," Mr. Hastings said. "I called my father this morning and he couldn't believe it. He was so happy he cried."

"That's only part of the story," Sheriff Weaver said. "We were able to open that safe this morning and had quite a shock."

"Was the money gone?" Josh asked.

"Oh, it was all there," Sheriff Barns said. "All $29,000 in cash. But that's not the best part."

"I've been looking at the coins and stamps that had been donated by Mr. Baniston," Mr. Finley said with great excitement. "He had a much more extensive and valuable collection than I ever imagined."

"What do you mean?" Carlos asked.

"Well, I was calculating rather quickly, but those rare stamps and coins are worth close to $400,000 by today's market prices and possibly more," Mr. Finley said. "They are in excellent shape and have increased greatly in value in thirty years."

"Over $400,000!" Josh said. All the other children's mouths dropped open in amazement.

"I think Springdale may get a shelter for those in need after all." Sheriff Weaver smiled.

The recovery of the stolen treasure got even more coverage in the *Springdale Gazette* than the rescue of Mr. Finley. The whole mood of the town seemed to change in just a few short days, as if an ancient dark cloud had been driven away.

"Home School Detectives Find 30-Year-Old Treasure!" was splashed across the headlines. Mrs. Highsmith's articles covered three whole pages in the *Springdale Gazette*. She told about Mr. Hastings's clearing his father's name, as well as about how the home school detectives had figured out the location of the treasure.

That Sunday afternoon, the Luke Fourteen Party given by the Springdale Community Church was a rousing success by any standards. By then, the whole town had heard about the missing treasure. Everyone was ready to celebrate.

After everyone ate, Pastor Brown read from 1 John 3:16-19.

"We know love by this, that He laid down his life for us: and we ought to lay down our lives for the brethren. But whoever has this world's goods, and beholds his brother in need and closes his heart against him, how does the love of God abide in him? Little children, let us not love with word or with tongue, but in deed and truth."

"We have many visitors today, and you are our honored guests," Pastor Brown said. "Over thirty years ago, the people in this community prayed and worked to help those in need. As we all know, that plan was interrupted by greedy men. But God did not forget the prayers of those in Springdale so long ago. And he has not forgotten our neighbors in need.

"Jesus died on the cross and rose again so that we would have salvation and hope. Eternal hope does not rest in our bank accounts or homes, yet the Lord has always been conscious of the very practical needs of our daily lives. In the same way, God has always been aware of the poor and needy throughout history. James tells us that it is pure religion to help the widows and the orphans.

"I don't know the answers for all the poor and homeless. Some people are just lazy or idle. Others have mental problems or drug addictions. Some are poor because fathers neglected to provide for their families. Some have been robbed of justice, like Mr. Hastings's father. Others just need jobs.

"Now Jesus said the poor would always be with us, but he didn't mean that as an excuse not to help those in need. He told us to love our neighbors as we love ourselves. Jesus' story of the good Samaritan is a plain example of what that means. If we think about the poor and homeless only as a large, complex problem, we may give up and not do anything. But I think Jesus wants you and me to see individuals around us as people, not problems.

"My prayer is that those who feel like strangers here today will find acceptance, love, and the grace of Jesus Christ and all the hope that he brings for the future. We want to welcome you as our neighbors to taste and see that God's grace is good."

Everyone applauded after the pastor spoke. Others lifted their hands in prayer and thanks. The party really took off then. Kids and adults played games, everybody ate more food, and then they gave out clothes and food to those who needed them.

Josh and the other home school detectives played their instruments for everyone. Mr. Walden beamed because they had never played better. After the classical compositions, the crowd wanted to sing praise songs. Josh and the others played with all their might. Even Billy got to beat the drums to his heart's content. No one cared whether or not he was too loud because Jesus was being praised, and he deserved a joyful noise.